RHYTHMIC

BLISS

Leigh Jarrett

Published by Steambath Press
An LJ M/M Romance

Paperback published September 2023
ISBN-13: 978-1-998008-20-9

Chapter One | Lucas

When the light turned off in the bathroom, a shiver ran up Lucas' spine. He didn't want to do this. It didn't happen often—the expectation of sex, but it came up at least once a week. His girlfriend had stuck around for 4 years, putting up with his indifference when it came to intimacy. He couldn't understand why Angie kept trying to spice things up in an attempt to coerce some interest.

He turned onto his side to watch her enter the bedroom. She was gorgeous, she really was. And sweet as the sugar coating on the rim of a White Lady or Sidecar cocktail. Lucas wasn't sure why Angie had stayed with him so long. They were more like semi-platonic best friends or roommates with occasional benefits. Not the loving romantic couple Angie wanted them to be.

In an effort to redeem himself and salvage the only long-term relationship he'd ever had, Lucas had asked Angie to marry him. They'd been engaged for 7 months with no wedding date marked on the calendar. He wasn't sure he could go through with it anyway—marrying Angie.

The uncertainty added to his chronic foul mood. Everything pissed him off. His day job in construction he was forced to go to even though he'd prefer to be playing music for a living. His boss, the asshole. His asinine co-workers whose only thought seemed to be fucking women.

He hated the fact that at the age of thirty-six, he was still in a cover band rather than an originals band. He hated his inability to find time to write his own music. Hated the buskers in downtown Victoria, BC strumming out their own originals and looking like they were having fun doing it. He hated crowds of tourists on the streets. Idiot drivers. Public arguments.

Just people in general.

The list went on and on.

And now Angie wanted to have sex. She was dressed in some sexy purple lingerie she had bought that afternoon. He had helped her pick it out. It did nothing for him.

He ran his hand through his hair.

Maybe I am impotent.

Angie had suggested going to a doctor to find out if his testosterone levels were low. He'd gone along with the idea and been told everything was fine. All should be in good working order.

Now, he was lying there naked, praying to God he could get an erection and keep it. Angie settled between his legs and took his cock into her mouth. She soon had it hard. That part wasn't a problem usually. Sometimes he couldn't get hard no matter what she did. Other times, his mind wandered and he was able to remove himself from the situation and just exist in the tactile world.

Tonight was a wandering night. He closed his eyes and thought about everything he could other than the fact Angie was sucking on his cock. The band. The audience. New song lyrics.

He opened his eyes when Angie released him and shifted. She moved until she was straddling his hips. She rocked back and forth on his hard cock with her pantie-covered pussy, her hands grasping either side of his belly. Rocking and sighing and moaning.

Lucas had to close his eyes again.

He wished he could close his ears.

The sounds and motion did nothing to keep him hard. It was more likely his erection would wane. He needed to stop her before she made him soft.

"Can you get off." Lucas grasped Angie's hips and guided her off. There was only one position he could do this in. He needed to have her on her knees. She knew the drill. She rolled off him and kneeled near the head of the bed. All he could see was her ass. He peeled off her panties as his heart rattled around in his chest. He felt a little panicky. Almost nauseous.

It had to be this way, her facing away from him. He didn't want to see her breasts bouncing to the motion of his thrusts. It was a turn-off. He didn't even want to see her face. If she looked into his eyes, she'd be able to tell in an instant he wasn't into this. That he was doing it for her.

He guided his cock to her vagina and reacquainted his cockhead with it. He so badly wanted to press into the hole above. Angie had only let him do it once and she had hated it. But it had felt so good to him. The perfect tightness and warmth. His cock had remained rock-hard throughout.

Lucas slid into her. She moaned and pushed back against him. He placed his hands on her hips and set a rhythmic pace. It was like keeping time with a drummer. Every thrust took up two beats. Three more and that completed 8 beats—a measure. Then he'd start again counting in 8s.

If he didn't think about what he was doing, he might be able to cum.

I'm so broken.

He pinched his eyes closed and steadied his breathing. When he was a teenager, he could have fucked and cum with anyone—anything. A girl, his fist, a pitted peach—anything. It wasn't until he hit his third year in university that he started having trouble. He reminisced back to that time.

Student party. Incredibly drunk. He'd found himself in a back hallway with a guy who had been eyeing him all night. Lucas had only been in search of the bathroom. The guy had followed him. He never did find out his name. While he waited for the bathroom to be available, the guy approached him. Didn't say a word. Just leaned in and kissed him.

Lucas hadn't pulled away. He'd explored what the guy was offering even cupping the guy's face to keep him in place. The only reason they'd stopped was the bathroom door swung open.

The guy had walked away and he'd never seen him again.

He allowed himself to drift back to that kiss. What it had done to his insides. The guy had been an amazing kisser. It had made him hard then. It made him hard now.

He continued his strokes into Angie and kept that kiss in his mind.

The taste—the feel; chasing every sensation as their tongues tangled.

The heat between them.

The guy's hard cock pressed against his.

His hole clenching with anticipation.

Yearning—aching.

Lucas grunted and spilled into Angie.

That guy had ruined him for every relationship he'd had after that. Nothing intimate had ever felt like that kiss again. Every time he thought about it, he longed for it to happen once more.

Just once—he only needed to experience it again once.

He slipped out of Angie and waited for her to flip over. He lay down beside her and ran his middle finger between her cum-slicked labia. She was already close. It wouldn't take long.

She gasped and sighed beside him, then trembled and convulsed. Despite his aversion, Lucas felt obligated to help her finish. It was the right thing to do. He was her fiancé after all.

Work sucked. But at least they had a gig tonight. It was Friday and the pubs downtown were always looking for live music. The Mike Waters Band was sought after. When they played, the dance floor was packed and well-lubricated with alcohol. They knew how to bring the party.

Lucas arrived an hour before the gig. It would take them a while to set up and do a sound check. The bass player was already there, adjusting his monitor and tuning his guitar.

Lucas stepped up on stage, guitar case and microphone carry bag in hand. He was the lead guitarist and lead vocalist. He had a bit more to figure out. He started with his guitar, plugged it into an amplifier, then positioned his microphone and mic stand, attached a cable to the mic, and plugged it into the mixing board. He took a few minutes, tuned his guitar, and checked his monitor to make sure his sound levels were good for the pub. In addition to his floor monitor, he had in-ear monitors. He only wore one and used it to focus on his voice.

He and the bass player played around and made sure there wasn't any feedback from their monitors. Lucas touched his overdrive pedal a few times to ensure it was in the right place. He didn't want to be looking for it in the middle of a song.

The two of them were all set and ready to go.

There was always one guy in a band who was late to everything. Their guy was the drummer. He was barely there in time to adjust the drum kit before they ran sound. It was the drummer's band though, so it's not like they could say anything. A friend of theirs from another band popped in and offered to set up their sound levels. It was a relief not having to do it himself.

Leaping on and off the stage. Adjusting volumes. Trading off the soundboard tablet with the bass player. Hoping to hell his own sound was good everywhere in the pub. It was better if someone else with more experience did it but not all pubs had their own sound techs.

This very popular pub right downtown on Government Street did not. It wasn't the best place to be on a Friday night but it paid well enough. Being a 3-piece band meant they'd each walk away with two hundred dollars in their pockets. Three nights a week of that and it was decent money.

Just not enough to make it his solitary income.

Once they were set, the girls all showed up. The drummer, Mike was married. So was the bass guitarist, Samuel. Lucas' Angie filled out the trio of groupies. At least once a week, they'd come to a show. The three women had become good friends with each other over the years.

Angie approached the stage. Lucas leaned down and kissed her. In public, they made a good show of it, looking like they were in love. Behind closed doors, they rarely touched each other.

The band began the sound check.

Lucas stepped up to his microphone. "Check. Check. Testing. Testing." A few song lyrics.

Thumbs up from their friend. "Samuel. Your mic."

Samuel sang a short chorus. Mike's mic was next.

"Just going to do a quick sound check," Lucas said to the audience and then they played the first half of one of their popular songs. They got a spattering of clapping.

They all hopped off the stage. They still had 15 minutes until they had to start. Enough time to down a beer and order another. Once it was time to start, Lucas brought his second beer up on stage with him and set it on the floor next to his all-important fan. The lights could get hot.

He adjusted his tablet on the mic stand. It had their suggested set lists on it and the words to each song in case he had a brain fart and forgot the lyrics. Never happened but he felt better having them there. He didn't always stick to the set list. He often gauged what they were going to play next on the crowd. Were they paying attention? Were there people on the dance floor?

"Hey, we're about to get started," Mike said to the audience through his microphone.

"We're The Mike Waters Band," Lucas continued. "And we're going to play you some rock classics tonight." He pointed at an empty, plastic water pitcher at the front of the stage. Their glass tip jar had been lost between gigs somehow. "And we have a tip jar if you're feeling generous." It didn't often amount to much. They usually walked away with ten dollars each.

The first set consisted of fourteen songs. Some people in the pub were barely listening. Never looked toward the stage; instead, they continued their conversations with people at their table.

Then there were the people who sat and listened and clapped after each song. And lastly, there was the enthusiastic crowd. Singing and dancing to the music. The third crowd gave them energy. Made all the practices worth it. The band schedule took up three to four evenings of Lucas' week.

It was a commitment. But they all loved playing music. Performing was infinitely better than being a weekend basement band just playing for their own enjoyment.

Lucas loved being on stage. Loved being the center of attention as the lead singer. All his annoyance with the world melted away. That version of Lucas on the stage was unrecognizable. His singing was full of emotion and he bantered with the band and joked with the audience.

He was never happier than when he was performing.

Lucas had a surprise for the band tonight. During the third set, a saxophone player jumped on stage and joined them for a few songs. The audience ate it up. Cheering and whistling. He'd found the guy through another band he knew, a friend of theirs only in town for a few days. He was well worth the fifty dollars Lucas would be paying him out of his own pocket.

By the time they finished for the night, Lucas was six beers in. It was 12:30. There were places to go to drink until 2 am. They packed up quickly, stored their gear in Mike's minivan, and went in search of some entertainment. They had an hour to get completely wasted.

Lucas liked drinking way too much on gig nights. Alcohol and seeing him on stage made Angie horny but by his being too drunk, he had a ready-made excuse.

Too drunk.

Too stressed out.

Too tired.

He'd used them all. They wandered into Deckers Pub at the bottom of the square. Loud music was pumping through the speakers. The dance floor was packed. The space around the tables was packed. They found a small place to stand near the bar. It made the acquisition of alcohol easier.

Angie hauled on Lucas' arm. "Let's dance."

He was too drunk to resist her insistence. He let himself be pulled onto the dancefloor. The beats were easy to follow. He usually wasn't into pop music but moving his body to it felt good. He stepped aside as a tall muscular guy angled his way through the crowd and jumped on stage to make sure the band that had been playing earlier in the night had stored everything correctly. Some bands were better than others at cleaning up after themselves.

Deckers had a dedicated sound person who also took care of the stage. Lucas liked playing there. It felt more professional. The Mike Waters Band was popular so they were hired to play there at least twice a month. They paid more than the other pubs as well. An extra $200.

And they paid in cash.

Angie wrapped her arms around Lucas' neck as a slower song came on. She tried to kiss him, but his attention was on the sound guy. He'd only seen the back of him so far, but his ass was tight and high; his legs long, And his hair a deep chocolate brown. Every once in a while he caught a glimpse of facial hair and black-rimmed glasses in his profile.

"What are you looking at?" Angie asked,

"Nothing," Lucas lied. "Just thought I knew that guy."

When the guy leaped off the stage, Lucas was able to get a good look at him. His heart stuttered a little. He was stunning. Gorgeous. All the good words rolled into one. The wide, natural smile the guy had on his face as he passed through the crowd drew all sorts of emotions out that had been buried for a long time. Lucas' stomach twisted as the guy headed toward the back of the pub.

Lucas grasped Angie's shoulders. "Be back in a minute."

He wasn't sure what possessed him but he needed to talk to the guy. Lucas found him at the back of the bar tucking away the soundboard tablet.

"Time to head out?" Lucas shouted at him above the loud

music.

The guy nodded. "Yeah. Long day." He raised his head. Behind his glasses, his hazel brown eyes surrounded by thick dark lashes blinked at Lucas and nearly dropped him. Up close, the guy was even more devastating to look at. He could feel a runaway, rapid pulse pound in his throat.

Fighting to recover, the guy's lips caught Lucas' attention as he flashed a smile at him. Pink and smooth as though they were specifically designed for joy. The smile made the corners of his eyes crinkle in a lovable way that felt like he'd known the guy all his life. In reality, he'd never seen him before. That was unusual. He'd thought he knew everybody.

He leaned forward and shouted.

"You new to the scene?"

"Just moved here two weeks ago!"

"From where?"

"Ottawa!"

"Ew! You'll find the weather here more agreeable!"

"One of the reasons I moved here!"

"You chose well!" Lucas scrolled through his mind looking for more questions he could ask. He wanted to get to know this guy. He was intrigued by him. "Do you do sound anywhere else?"

"This is the first job I've picked up so far but the guy who runs the sound here has promised to get me into a few more places!"

Lucas nodded. "Good! It's all about who you know in this town!"

"I've figured that out! It's a smaller scene than Ottawa! Tighter knit by the looks of it!"

"Everybody knows almost everybody! Or they've heard of you!"

The guy held out his hand. "In that case, I'm Nick!"

Lucas prepared himself to touch Nick's skin. He shook his hand as firmly as he dared. A shower of little sparks shot straight up his arm. "I'm Lucas! Lead singer of The Mike Waters Band!"

"You played up at the top of the square tonight!"

"That was us!"

"I caught half of your first set! Pretty sweet!"

"Thanks!"

"You do it full-time?"

"I wish!"

A song came on that shook the floor with thunderous sound. Lucas recognized it from the radio station Angie insisted on listening to.

"Pretty hard to do!" Nick shouted.

"What?" He hadn't heard Nick above the music.

Nick leaned closer to Lucas' ear. His warm breath rolled across Lucas' cheek.

"Pretty hard to do!" he repeated.

The two words, "Pretty hard," were all that stuck in his head. Nick's breath tickled his jawline. Nick was waiting for an answer, but Lucas' cock had stirred. He was busy trying to figure that out.

He was too drunk to get an erection.

"Lucas?" Nick shouted.

Lucas brought himself back. "Sorry. I've had too much to drink!"

"You need a ride home?"

If he'd been alone, he would have jumped at it. A ride with Nick. They could talk more. Share what bands they were interested in. Have a few moments of silence with him.

Back to reality.

"No, I took a cab with my girlfriend!"

Nick's eyebrows peaked. "You have a girlfriend?"

"Yeah ... why?"

Nick shook his head. "Nothing! I just got a single vibe off of you!"

And this is where things went off the rails.

"Probably will be again soon!" Lucas shouted. He wasn't sure where that had come from. He hadn't even given it any thought yet—breaking up with Angie.

"Relationship problems?"

"Just not into it anymore! Haven't been for a while!"

God, I really am drunk.

"Sorry to hear that!"

"It's been a long 4 years!"

Nick leaned on the bartop. "Why didn't you leave her sooner?"

Lucas shrugged. "Afraid to be alone, I guess!"

Nick frowned at him. "The music is really loud in here! Can we talk out front?" Lucas nodded and Nick started walking through the hordes of people toward the front door.

Lucas checked over his shoulder as he passed the dance floor. Angie was laughing and talking to the other two women they had come with. He'd come back and find her later.

It really was quieter outside. He followed Nick along the front of the building a few feet. Nick leaned against the brick wall. His eyes watched every step Lucas made toward him.

"Better?" Nick asked.

"I can hear myself think."

Nick smiled. "Sometimes that can be a bad thing."

"True." The fresh air shocked his brain a little. It was a nice night for March, but it was cold standing outside without a jacket. His thoughts began forming more logically.

"Sorry for laying all that on you," Lucas said.

"You obviously needed it off your chest."

"But we just met. I shouldn't have done it."

Nick crossed his arms against the cold. "No worries. Not like I'm going to tell anyone." He rocked back and forth, bumping his ass against the wall. "You really going to break up with her?"

Lucas scrubbed a hand through his hair.

No idea.

"I don't know. We've been together for a long time. It's the longest relationship I've ever had."

"Started out good?"

Lucas coughed out a laugh. "It's always been strained." He was not going to tell this guy he just met that he hated having sex with his girlfriend. He wasn't that drunk.

"Maybe someday you'll find someone you click with right away."

"Wouldn't that be nice." Lucas looked up into the night sky. The only person he'd *clicked with right away* in a long time was this guy. It was easy to talk to him.

Nick pushed away from the wall. "Well, I gotta go." He held out his hand to Lucas. "It was nice meeting you, Lucas. Maybe we'll see each other around."

Lucas shook Nick's hand. This time it was pure warmth that crawled up his arm. His cock stirred for the second time that night. "Yeah. You too. Have a good night."

His gaze followed Nick as he headed back inside. It made him feel fuzzy to watch him. He could've talked to him for longer. So much longer. He was about to go back in through the front doors when the entourage he'd come with came squealing out of the pub.

"Oh, here you are!" Angie latched onto him and hugged

him. "Mike said he saw you go outside." She tousled his hair. "What are doing out here?"

Mike handed Lucas his coat.

"Just talking to someone," Lucas answered. "The sound guy. Interesting guy. Nick."

"Yeah," Samuel said. "He's new. Supposed to be good. Has his own sound studio."

"Like where he lives?" Mike asked.

"Yeah, he lives in a house with some other musicians out in Esquimalt somewhere. Can't imagine his neighbors are thrilled."

The wheels began to roll in Lucas' mind. Knowing someone with a sound studio was a step toward recording and releasing his own music. "Does he work here every Friday night?"

"Don't know," Samuel said. "Doubt it. He just started."

Lucas stared in through the doors of the pub. He so badly wanted to go back in there and hunt Nick down. To find out more about his studio. To exchange numbers.

Anything to talk to him again.

He turned away from the door when his friends hailed a couple of cabs. As they drove away, Nick exited the pub. He caught sight of Lucas through the window of the cab and waved at him.

Lucas waved back, then slumped down in his seat next to Angie. The urge to leap out of the cab and go after Nick was fierce. Angie reached for his hand and he took it. The simple act reminded him of everything he had said to Nick about his relationship with her.

He needed to talk to Angie.

They couldn't keep dragging this thing through the mud any longer.

Chapter Two | Nick

As usual, for a Tuesday it was a busy night. Most pubs and bars had what they called *Industry Night* on a Tuesday so there were lots of people walking past his busking area. Not only did they throw money into his guitar case, but they often hung around to talk to him.

It wasn't just restaurant employees out on a Tuesday night, it was other musicians. Service industry people often made friends with the bands that played at their workplaces. They hung out together on a Tuesday and sought out the solo and duo acts playing mid-week.

A few people in bands had collected Nick's contact information, promising to bring him on stage as a guest next week. Those were the kind of breaks he needed even though he'd continue busking. He loved the freedom of being able to play his original music.

Nick was on a break and scrolling through his phone, looking at a set list a guy had sent him for their band. He was to pick out three or four songs he could jump in on. There were plenty of 3-piece bands that were happy to have a rhythm guitar player as a guest.

A guy who played solo on the music scene took his number as well. He wanted to have choices of people to call if he needed someone to fill in when he couldn't make a gig for some reason. Those gigs were all over the place, from downtown to the edge of Metchosin.

Luckily, Nick had bought a car as soon as he moved here. He'd been in Victoria for just over a month. It was starting to feel like home. He'd spent a significant amount of time wandering downtown and driving around, trying to figure out the lay of the roads.

Some city planners had gone crazy with one-way streets.

And roads that changed names like three times.

A noisy bunch of guys stumbled down the street as he played the start of the last song of his third and final set. They came to a stop in front of him to listen. He recognized the big guy out front. He was the drummer of the band he had caught a couple of songs of two weeks ago.

As he sang and strummed, Nick scanned the crowd. There were at least ten of them.

This is his band.

The Mike Waters Band.

Lucas' band.

He might be here. He nearly fucked up his rhythm when at the back, he caught a glimpse of the face that had been haunting his dreams. Lucas was looking around as if he wanted to leave.

Then Lucas decided to glance at who was playing the music. At first, he looked annoyed and then he looked straight at Nick. His eyes grew wide. Then his brow furrowed.

He looked pissed off.

Not the look he had hoped Lucas would give him someday.

The song came to a close and Nick smiled at the crowd of listeners. "That's it for me for the night. I'm here every Tuesday and Thursday night."

The majority of the people shifted. The drummer he had identified approached him. "You ever play with a full band?"

"I played with a band in Ottawa," Nick said. "Pretty popular one too."

"Cover band?"

"Yeah. Rock, Pop, R&B … the whole gamut."

"Would you be interested in guesting with us sometime?"

"Absolutely. Always looking for more work."

"Eight songs and we'd pay you $50."

"Sounds good." That was really good money. Like crazy good. The guy must have been impressed with him. The guy looked over his shoulder. "Lucas, come here. We need you to coordinate with this guy." He looked at Nick. "What's your name?"

"Nick Cartright."

The guy extended his hand. "I'm Mike. The Mike Waters Band is mine."

Lucas wandered up beside Mike. Nick watched Lucas' eyes. They were studying Nick's entire presence from his hair to his shoes. His gaze came to rest on Nick's eyes.

There was a spark of something there.

Just as there had been at the pub.

"Could you talk to Nick for a few minutes?" Mike asked Lucas. "Exchange contact information. Figure out what songs he might be able to play with us."

"Sure thing."

"We'll see you at Deckers."

With the band and their entourage heading down the square, silence descended around them other than a few people talking as they passed by. Nick watched Lucas contemplate his next sentence. His dark blond hair was down tonight. It hung level with his jawline. His facial hair was the length Nick liked. Not so short it was abrasive. Not so long that you could run your fingers through it. Just enough to caress your balls and the crease of your ass.

"So, you're a busker," Lucas said.

"That would be why I'm standing here."

"I hate buskers."

Wow. Okay.

"And why would that be?"

"It's so easy for you out here."

"Easy how?" Lucas was gravely mistaken. His sets were all originals. Writing, practicing, and performing sets of what he'd created was hard work.

"You're doing all originals."

"Yeah," Nick replied. Lucas hadn't answered his question. *Easy how?* God, the scowl on the guy was vicious. It was possible he was even gritting his teeth.

"That's why," Lucas said.

"Because I sing originals … you think that's easy? And you hate it?" It suddenly dawned on him what Lucas' problem was with him. "You hate doing cover work, don't you?"

"Hate is a strong word. I have fun doing what I'm doing."

"But you want to do more."

Lucas' face relaxed. "I have lots of ideas. Pages and pages of them."

"And you want to put them to music?"

"I've written most of the music already."

"Why haven't you approached your band about them?"

"It's not my band. It's Mike's. He doesn't want originals *mucking things up*."

"So you want to record them instead?"

"That's the dream."

"I can help you with that. I almost have my studio set up."

The idea of having Lucas in his home, working on music, made his heart rate speed up a little. They'd be spending a lot of time together in close quarters.

A slight lift of Lucas' left cheek meant he'd almost smiled. He'd like to be the one to make Lucas really smile. Smile and squirm and moan beneath his touch.

"I'd like that." Lucas handed Nick his phone. "Let's exchange contact info."

Nick handed Lucas his phone and typed his information into Lucas' phone. "Are you sure you want to be working with a busker?" He smiled at Lucas and gave him back his phone.

"Depends. How much are you going to be charging me?"

"We'll work out something reasonable." To be honest, he would do it for free if it meant he could spend more time with this scowly guy. There had to be some joy in there somewhere.

He looked at what Lucas had typed into his phone. Lucas Peterson. That name would be on his mind every time Lucas' face drifted into his thoughts. He'd never met anyone with such a permanently angry face. When he *imagined* it, Lucas' face was undone by ecstasy.

Nick cleared his throat. "So, how are things going since the last time I saw you?"

Lucas turned his head, gazing down the dark street. "Broke up with her."

Nick thought his breath was going to stumble over his heart's pounding. Lucas was no longer in a relationship that wasn't the right fit for him. He wondered if Lucas would ever figure out what the right fit would be for him. And would he be brave enough to pursue it.

"How did that go?"

Lucas snorted. "She was relieved."

"Ouch."

"No, it wasn't right … us together. Right from the start."

Nick set his guitar in its case and closed it up. "I'm sorry to hear that. 4 years is a long time to be with a person who isn't right for you."

Lucas' eyebrows rose as he turned to face Nick. Yes, he'd remembered that Lucas had said it was a 4-year relationship. He'd remembered everything Lucas had said to him.

"You remembered that?"

Nick shrugged. "You made an impression."

Lucas sighed as he stared at Nick. The spark of interest was still there in his eyes. It was too soon to tell if Lucas would let it grow. Right now, he seemed to be trying to control it.

The spark of interest won out.

"Do you want to grab a quiet bite to eat?" Lucas asked. "I think the cheesecake place is still open. Or we could go somewhere else."

"Cheesecake sounds good."

Lucas took Nick's rolled cable and amplifier to help out and they headed down the street. It was only a few blocks and up some stairs. Franko's was one of the few restaurants serving food this late at night. There was a curry place too but it was on the other side of downtown.

They seated themselves near the window.

Lucas pulled out his phone. "I'm sending you our set list."

Nick scanned through it. "I know most of these songs on here."

"Were you lead or rhythm?"

"Lead."

"Pick four and learn the rhythm part of them. Then let me know what they are."

"I appreciate the opportunity. I want to play in a band again."

"You need to meet more people. Make sure you stick around on breaks and after the show."

Nick leaned back in his seat. Most of the grumpiness had

drained out of Lucas' face. Talking about playing music soothed the beast in him. Note taken.

"When did you start playing music?" Nick asked.

"Picked up my first guitar at nine."

"Ten for me." Nick smiled at him, deliberately. He liked how Lucas' gaze was drawn to his lips when he smiled. He was certain there was something there. "Wrote your first song?"

"Started writing rudimentary poetry when I was seven or eight. They were crap but I loved doing it. Started setting them to music when I was twelve or so."

"I was a late bloomer. Didn't get into writing music until I was in my 20s."

Lucas smirked. The closest damned thing that had come anywhere near being a smile. He wanted to make him do it again. "My first few attempts were rubbish."

Lucas smirked again. It seemed he found Nick's failures amusing. Lucas must really hate buskers. Surely, he'd be given a free pass, though. They were clicking like a roll of bubble wrap.

"I should let you hear them," Nick continued.

This statement earned a quiet laugh from Lucas. There was a warm human being in there somewhere. "I'll load them up when you come to my place," Nick added.

Lucas caught his gaze. "That would bring me a great amount of pleasure."

God damn.

There were infinitely more things that he could do to Lucas that would bring him a great amount of pleasure. Like Lucas' legs wrapped around his hips as he pounded him into his mattress.

Then sucking Lucas to climax.

Nick coughed, nearly choking on the spit collecting in his

mouth as his mouth watered for a taste of Lucas' cock. Recovered and curious, he caught Lucas' gaze and licked his lips.

Lucas cleared his throat.

Nick blinked, slowly, judging Lucas' reaction. Lucas was breathing hard as he stared at Nick. This time there was hunger in his eyes. Nick needed to steer the conversation back to music before they ended up in a back alley somewhere and completely freaked Lucas out.

He didn't want to scare Lucas off by plunging him headfirst into his obvious craving.

"What kind of music do you write?" Nick asked.

"Blues and a bit of R&B."

"I'm a soft rock guy."

"Figured that out by what you were playing tonight."

The hunger disappeared behind a shield. Nick was sad to see it go. It had been a while since someone had desired him that heavily. If they had, he hadn't been paying attention. His focus was usually on his music. The sidelines of his life whirred past him in a blur.

But this guy here, Lucas … he'd caught his eye.

And it seemed to be mutual.

"When do you want to meet up?" Nick asked. "I can have my studio ready in a few days."

"How's next Monday? I get off work at 4. We can order a pizza and lay down some tracks."

"Sounds perfect." Nick texted Lucas his address. He was lucky to have found a house with a few other musicians. There was already a drum kit in a practice area and enough spare space in the basement for him to set up his recording equipment.

They ordered their cheesecake and fed themselves

mouthfuls in between naming off bands and songs that were their favorites. Nick told Lucas about his recording equipment. How he got started. Which bands had done album recordings with him. Even told him he'd done some voice work as a narrator for books. He deliberately failed to mention they were gay erotica books.

He could make his voice sound smooth and sultry and he knew it.

Lucas told him who in the Victoria music scene he needed to become friendly with. Who was easy to let along with. Who was not. Who to avoid.

It was a complete flood of information but Nick was good that way, remembering stuff. You needed to be when you were memorizing what amounted over the years to hundreds of songs.

Lucas snagged the bill before Nick had a chance to grab it.

"This one is mine."

Nick smiled at him. "Are we going to do this again?"

"No. You can buy me a drink or two when you play with us."

A scowl and a complete shutdown. Lucas was fighting hard against the pull between them. The possibility of getting Lucas to act on the percolating desire probably wasn't worth pursuing.

Nick rose to his feet. "Will do. Let me know when that is. Meanwhile, I'll see you on Monday."

"What time? 5:30?"

"Works for me."

Not even a handshake, Lucas climbed out of the booth seating and left without even looking back at him. The last time their hands had made contact, it had been electrifying. Nick knew Lucas had felt it too. He'd seen it in his expression.

Absolute shock. It was no wonder Lucas didn't want the handshake to happen again. The guy was in complete and utter denial.

Monday rolled around—slowly. Nick had everything set up. He'd even changed out the lightbulbs in the basement and put down a carpet so it wasn't so dreary down there.

His phone lit up with a text. For a brief second, he thought it might be Lucas canceling. Instead, it was Lucas telling him he had arrived.

Nick raced upstairs and opened the front door. Lucas slammed the door of his huge, black pickup truck and wandered up the walkway with a guitar case in his hand.

He nodded at Nick.

"Nick."

"Hey, Lucas. Come on in. We'll be working downstairs in the basement." He shut the door as Lucas crowded into the front entry. "Can I get you anything to drink before we get started?"

"Water would be good."

"I'll get that for you." Nick pointed down the stairs. "Head down and to your left."

Nick watched Lucas walk down the stairs. He had some of his hair pulled into a knot at the back of his head with a blue, twisty, coated hair tie. Stepping through the front door, Lucas' pulled-back hair had showed off his sharp jawline. Nick hummed softly. He wanted to sink his teeth into it. Feel the bristles of Lucas' beard crackling against the back of his incisors.

He went to the kitchen for two glasses of ice water. When he arrived in the studio, Lucas was tuning his guitar. He set both glasses on top of an old coffee table he had hauled down there.

He needed to sit. His cock had chubbed up a bit while thinking about attacking Lucas. They weren't going to get anything done if he kept lusting after the guy.

Backburner.

Nick had already set everything up for them to jump right in.

"We're going to start by doing a demo track of each song. Then play around with them next time we meet up." He checked what Lucas was doing. He'd figured out where to plug in his guitar.

"I guess we start with a guitar track?" Lucas asked.

"Right. Then you can sing over each one. Don't get too hung up on details. This is just a first go-around. These tracks can be stripped out when we lay down the real material."

Nick handed Lucas a set of headphones. "So you can hear yourself."

Lucas put them on and strummed his guitar a few times. He looked up and nodded at Nick, letting him know he was ready. Nick put his headphones on and counted Lucas in.

He'd add an electronic drum line in once he'd heard Lucas' guitar line.

Nick lightly touched a few levels as Lucas began playing. The song was wrapped around some classic R&B guitar stylings. Lucas was really good. He could see why his band was so popular.

He got swept up in it, riding every strum and finger-pick. It was a beautiful piece of music. Lucas brought the song to a close and Nick stopped the recording.

Both Nick and Lucas lifted one side of their headphones off.

"Vocals next." Nick swung the microphone down in front

of Lucas and adjusted it to be the right height. "Just test it for me first."

Lucas set his errant headphone back on his ear. "Check. Check. Test. Test."

"Sound good to you?"

Lucas gave him a thumbs up.

Nick ran the guitar track and Lucas jumped in. The song was about heartache, misunderstanding, and not knowing if the right person existed in the world for you.

Nick sat back and watched Lucas. His voice was exquisite. The lyrics were haunting and raw. They exposed so much of what Lucas was feeling or must have felt at one point in his life.

The mindset of the person who wrote those words made Nick sad. His gaze wandered over Lucas. He was hurting. And he was lost. There was a real heart beating below the surface of Lucas' outward appearance of annoyance and disgruntlement. And it had no idea where it wanted to go.

The words ended. The guitar track played out. And he stopped the recording.

"Let's listen back," Nick said.

Lucas closed his eyes and pressed the headphones to his ears. He tapped his foot to every beat of the song. Nick just watched him. The urge to touch Lucas as he was taken on a journey through his recorded lyrics nearly lifted Nick from his chair. He wanted to comfort him. To take away all the pain he'd exposed with those words he'd written. Nick jammed a bent knuckle against his eye to stop an unruly tear that threatened to escape down his cheek.

The track ended and Lucas pulled the headphones off his ears. Nick did the same.

"What do you think?" Nick asked.

"I'd like to add some harmony."

"For sure … yeah." Nick cleared his throat. "I can add the drum line later."

They did five songs in total that evening. Decided to stop when the grumbling of their stomachs threatened to make it through onto the recordings.

"What kind of pizza do you want?" Nick asked. "We can eat and then do another song."

"Preferably one with lots of meat on it. I'm not into that veggie stuff."

"I'm with you on that. Pepperoni and ground beef galore it is."

"So what happens next with the recordings?"

"I play around with them. Make them sound pretty." Nick typed into a pizza delivery app on his phone. A large meat lover pizza. And a medium pepperoni and bacon. "I'll send you the files as I finish them so you can have a listen." He led Lucas upstairs to the living room. You could hear his roommates practicing music in their rooms. Two guitars and a keyboard. It was past 11. The guys would have eaten already. No need to loop them in on the pizza.

"Really appreciate this," Lucas said. "How much am I going to owe you per song?"

"I'll make sure you can afford it. Let's not get into money yet."

Nick dropped onto the sofa. Lucas took a seat at the far opposite end of the sofa from him.

So, it's going to be like that, is it?

"You thought about dating yet?" Nick asked.

Jump right the fuck in.

A crimson flush crawled up Lucas' neck and stopped at the lobes of his ears. He kept looking straight ahead. Nick turned to face him, placed an elbow on the back of the sofa, and propped his head on his hand. He was curious how far he could push Lucas.

"Hadn't thought about it," Lucas answered.

"Just haven't met the right person."

"I don't end up talking to many people."

"But you're the lead singer of a band. Surely, you're approached."

"I don't want to go out with any of those women. Especially ones that follow our band. Starting a relationship atop someone else's pedestal is a recipe for disappointment."

Nick chewed his bottom lip, then barged ahead.

"Do men ever approach you?"

Now, Lucas turned to look at him. The muscle in his jaw twitched. Maybe he'd pushed too hard. But Nick wanted to know how Lucas handled those male advances.

"Sometimes."

"And what do you say to them?"

"That I'm not interested."

"Are you telling the truth?"

Lucas scowled at him. "Of course, I am."

Caution to the damned wind.

"If they asked me, I would be lying if I said I wasn't interested."

More scowling. More blinking. Moments ticked by.

"You're gay?" Lucas asked at last.

"Bisexual."

Lucas grunted and stared off across the room. "I wouldn't have guessed that."

"You don't think I give off that kind of vibe?"

Lucas would be telling lies if he answered no to that question. They'd *both* felt it in the cheesecake restaurant. That yearning for each other. He'd done nothing to hide it from Lucas.

"Maybe."

Ah, so he did notice.

The app on Nick's phone dinged. The pizza had been made and it was on its way. They had another fifteen minutes until this conversation would be interrupted.

"Is that why you were staring at me at the restaurant? You picked up on the vibe."

Lucas whipped his head around and stared at Nick. Seriously deep scowl going on. It made his eyes dark and creases broke out across his forehead. He looked on the verge of exploding with anger. That wasn't Nick's intention. He hadn't meant to elicit that kind of reaction.

Lucas was deeper in the closet than he'd realized.

"I was what?" Lucas growled.

"You were staring." Nick shuffled a little closer to Lucas on the sofa. "I don't mind. You were doing the same thing at Deckers." He was taking his damned life in his hands.

But he couldn't stop himself.

Lucas swallowed hard. "I think I should go."

"Pizza hasn't arrived yet."

"Suddenly, I'm not hungry."

Nick lifted himself off the sofa and sat next to Lucas. He had never in his life been this forward. Especially with someone this volatile. He didn't go as far as to touch him. Even though he desperately wanted to. "Why? Because it's possible you might be interested?"

"I have no interest in men."

"Huh." Nick looked down into Lucas' lap. Their conversation and Nick's proximity to Lucas had made Lucas' cock hard. The mass in Lucas' jeans looked as if it was aching to be released.

Lucas caught him looking.

"Please don't," Lucas said. "It doesn't mean anything."

"If you say so." Nick moved back to his end of the sofa. He'd pried all the answers out of Lucas he needed. Whatever Lucas' sexuality, there was a connection between the two of them.

Now, what to do with that.

Chapter Three | Lucas

Lucas was glad Nick had offered him a beer to go with the pizza. He was feeling stressed. He still wasn't sure why he had stayed. Nick had practically accosted him.

Mentally at least.

He had been on the verge of blowing up at Nick and storming out. Except, everything Nick said happened, happened. He *had* been staring at Nick across that table. The blinking of Nick's lashes, the shape of his mouth as he spoke—it had been mesmerizing.

But he wasn't into guys.

He was surprised Nick was. He never would have pegged Nick as bisexual. Not that he knew what a guy who also liked guys looked like. Nick looked like everyone else on the music circuit. Not the greatest clothes even on stage. Jeans, worn-out band t-shirts, and messy hair.

At least his hygiene wasn't questionable like so many.

In fact, he smelled amazing. When Nick had moved down the sofa and sat beside him, Lucas had breathed in the scent of him. A small part of him had wanted Nick to touch him.

To touch his shoulder. Lay his hand on his thigh.

Cup his thickening cock.

Lucas cleared his throat. "Sorry, what?" He'd missed what Nick was saying.

"I was asking what other venues I should be contacting."

"I'll text you a list. Plus some numbers of booking agents."

"Appreciated."

"Should we record one more song?"

Nick looked at his phone. "It's almost midnight. Do you work in the morning?"

"I'll call in sick."

"Where do you work?"

"Tyndale Construction. We're working on that building by the old bus station on Douglas." Lucas cleaned his pizza fingers on a napkin. "Been doing it for fourteen years."

Nick leaned back. "No wonder you're so muscular. I thought you worked out."

"No need to work out when you're doing that kind of work."

"No, I guess not." Nick had a wistful look in his eyes. It pulled at Lucas' heart a little. He preferred when Nick's eyes were cheerful and full of life.

"What's wrong?"

"I don't know." Nick shook his head. "I'm just tired."

"I'll come back another time. It's late."

Nick reached out and grabbed Lucas' wrist. "I'd prefer if you stayed a while longer." The wistful look was gone. This look … this was the look Nick had given Lucas in the restaurant.

Burning desire.

Lucas' cock stirred.

The urge to chase the flash of desire had Lucas hesitating. He rose to his feet. This wasn't who he was. Any fleeting, misguided appeal Nick had would completely disappear over time.

"I'm going," he said.

Nick sighed. "All right. Text me when you want to come back. I busk on Tuesday and Thursday night and do sound next Friday. I'll get those files ready for you."

"Let's do next Wednesday."

Nick smiled but it was weak, as if he was exhausted. "I'll pencil you in."

Away from the house, Lucas climbed into his truck. Nick waved at him from his door, then closed it. That expression on Nick's face … it wasn't exhaustion in his eyes.

It was defeat.

Nick had made a risky play for him to stay with him and he'd turned him down.

Jeezus.

His cock had been hard and he'd dismissed the person who caused it to pay attention for a change. He covered his eyes with one hand, then lowered it and pinched the bridge of his nose.

An advance from a guy.

A guy who had made him hard. Twice. In one night.

Angie had never had a record like that.

No girl ever had.

What the hell does that even mean?

I don't want to be gay.

He'd grown up in a small town at the north end of Vancouver Island. Men dated and married women. No deviation. Sure, there had been the odd queer kid in high school but they all moved away after graduation. Much like he had. His mind drifted back to that kiss at university.

That guy had made him hard.

Angie had fought every week to get a reaction from his cock. All that university guy had to do was kiss him. All Nick had to do was look at him with desire in his eyes.

He'd never considered it. That he might not be straight. He'd been playing with the idea that he was asexual. Every relationship he'd been in had retained the same sexual apathy throughout. It was always a struggle to get and stay hard. It was the reason Angie had been his only long-term relationship. Women just didn't do it for him.

He'd assumed no one did.

Except for that one guy in university.

And this guy … Nick. He'd been attracted to Nick since the first night he set eyes on him. Moth to a flame kind of shit. If he hadn't raced to the back of the bar to talk to him that night, he might have had a full-blown anxiety attack. The draw to talk to him had been extreme.

I don't want to be gay.

He looked at Nick's front door.

What would it mean if he went to him and found out the extent of his body's reaction to the guy? Nick turned him on. It was that simple. His cock swelled as he pictured him in his mind.

The third time in one night.

The guy had made him hard three times.

Fuck it.

Only one way to find out.

He climbed out of his truck and strode to the door. It was late, he didn't want to ring the doorbell or knock and wake up everyone. He retrieved his phone and sent Nick a text message.

<Lucas: I'm outside.>

<Nick: I know.>

<Lucas: No. I'm outside your door.>

<Nick: Why? Did you forget something?>

<Lucas: Yeah. You.>

Two seconds later, the door flung open. Lucas had to focus to breathe. He'd never been so terrified in his life. He let Nick make the first move. Nick clung to the front of Lucas' coat and dragged him into the house. One second he was in the doorway, the next second Nick slammed Lucas against the front entry wall and captured Lucas' mouth with warm, hungry lips.

Lucas groaned and embraced Nick. One hand on his back—the other on his ass, clutching Nick to him as if he'd be able to help him sort through the confusion and realization launching a war in his head. Eventually, realization won out. He met and returned every one of Nick's advances. Lips and tongues pursuing each other—again and again.

Nick's lips felt *so* good.

Nick deepened his attack. He reached behind him, removed Lucas' hands from touching his body, and pinned them to either side of Lucas' face. Lucas shuddered with arousal. He liked being restrained like that. Restrained and made to give up everything he knew about himself.

Nick retreated from Lucas' lips and smiled at him, then dove back in. Lucas nearly crumpled as Nick pressed his thigh between Lucas' legs.

Lucas couldn't help but grind his hard cock against it.

Nick moaned into his mouth. The sound vibrated in Lucas' throat. He chased after it. Seeking it out with his tongue. Nick laughed against his lips and pulled away.

"Fuck … I am *so* glad you came back," Nick said.

"Took me a few minutes to think about it."

"And what did you decide?"

Lucas squirmed against Nick's thigh. He flexed and unflexed his hands in Nick's grasp. There was only one answer to that question. "That I want you."

Nick bit Lucas' bottom lip, pulled it away from his gums, and released it.

"I was hoping you'd come to that conclusion."

"You knew."

"From the moment our eyes met at Deckers."

"I wasn't sure. I'm not into guys."

"You sure about that?"

Lucas looked at Nick's lips. He wanted them all over his body. Like the unknown guy in university. He'd dreamed of having every piece of his skin touched by those lips.

Nick released one of Lucas' hands and cupped Lucas' hard cock. He ground the heel of his hand against it, massaging the stiff length. "You've never dreamed about a guy doing this to you?"

Lucas groaned, shivered, and tipped his head back. "Once … one guy."

"What about this?" Nick unbuttoned Lucas' jeans and unzipped them. Lucas' knees threatened to abandon him as Nick slipped his hand into Lucas' underwear and grabbed his hard cock.

"Yes," Lucas gasped. "That."

His whole body quivered, vibrating. Nick's hand glided over his cock, tugging on it ever so softly, infuriating him. He dug the fingers of his freed hand into Nick's hair.

"Do you like that?" Nick teased.

"Harder."

"Mm … Lucas likes it rough."

Lucas grunted and grabbed a handful of Nick's hair when Nick increased his pace and the ferocity of his grip on Lucas' cock. Each tug nearly lifted Lucas' heels off the floor.

Fuck.

He was so turned on. And so close to cumming. Nick's strong, thick guitarist fingers wrapped around his cock were taking him to places he never knew existed.

"Hey!" A loud voice from the top of the stairs. "New guy! Take it to your room!"

The interruption startled Lucas back to reality.

Nick slipped his hand out of Lucas' pants. "Let's go to my room."

Lucas looked up the staircase at the fuming guy up there. He recognized him. He played in a country band. A standing downtown gig. Embarrassment flushed Lucas' cheeks. He didn't want to be here anymore. This was wrong. This wasn't him. He couldn't do this.

I don't want to be gay.

"No." Lucas shook his head. "I'm gonna go."

Nick's brows dipped. Sadness filled his eyes. He released Lucas' other hand. "Why?"

"This isn't me."

"You didn't like it?"

Lucas flicked his gaze to the top of the stairs. The guy was gone. "It doesn't mean anything. I'm a guy. Things naturally turn me on. That doesn't mean I want to follow through on them."

Nick took a step back. "Okay. I thought we had something."

"You're a great guy, Nick. I'm just not bisexual … gay … whatever."

Nick crossed his arms. "I'm going to stretch into your personal life here, but why was your relationship with your girlfriend *strained*? Was it because you couldn't perform?"

What the fuck?

"None of your damned business." He pushed past Nick and opened the front door. How the hell had Nick figured that out? He looked over at his shoulder at Nick.

He wasn't sure he wanted to walk away from him.

Nick put his hand on Lucas' shoulder.

"Come to my room. Let's figure this out together. We can just talk if you want."

Every breath of Lucas's dragged in and out, his chest

heaving. His heart was pounding. He wanted to reach out and touch Nick. He wanted to kiss him again.

That decided it.

I don't want to be gay.

"I'm sorry, but I have to go."

Lucas was miserable the rest of the week. Not an unusual state of being for him but this time, the reason was plaguing him. Asleep and awake. He couldn't get the feel of Nick's lips off his mind.

His lips. His strong hands. The overall bulk of his body as he'd pressed him to that wall. The pure maleness of him. His scent, his touch—his ability to arouse him.

Lucas poured himself his second coffee of the morning. He was going to be a few minutes late for work. Nick's words had his mind spinning. *Was it because you couldn't perform?* In Nick's hand, there had been nothing wrong with the performance of his cock to stay hard.

He could've cum like that. Pinned against the wall … Nick's hand down his pants.

He groaned and swept his hair off his forehead. He didn't want to accept the possibility he might not be heterosexual. It had been his identity his entire adult life.

I don't want to be gay.

He scrolled through mental images of the women he had been with over the years. Those he could remember. How many of those encounters had ended with him not being able to get it up?

Way too many.

Fuck.

Most.

Lucas poured his coffee into an insulated to-go mug. He

could drink it in the truck on his way to work. He was off to another 8 hours of putting up with his coworkers' bullshit.

He wasn't anything like them. Toxic male behavior oozed easily from them. He had more respect for women than they did … women just didn't interest him.

Lucas slammed his truck door.

Women don't interest you.

That was a revelation. It would explain so much of what he had gone through over the years. Failed relationships. Disappointing hookups. Not being able to find that one person who fit.

I don't want to be gay.

He started his truck and backed out of his driveway. It was a short drive to the worksite. His thoughts were occupied the entire time. He was opposed to labeling himself with an identity.

Of course, the road was filled with idiots. He spent half his drive laying on his horn. Two cars almost side-swiped him. Another was driving so slowly that he thought he was going backward.

He found a spot and parallel parked. He didn't feel gay. He'd never found himself drawn to men. He would have lusted after guys if he was gay, right?

I don't want to be gay.

Lucas avoided the other guys at work as best he could, keeping his head down and working. During lunch break, he found a quiet spot, pulled out a set of earbuds, and listened to the tracks Nick had sent him yesterday. He'd listened to them on a loop many times. Both because he enjoyed what he had laid down and because Nick's signature was all over them.

He could imagine Nick playing through his lyrics again and again, getting an inside look into what his aching heart was going through. His struggles. His heartbreak. His loneliness.

Maybe it would be enough to scare Nick off.

The sun broke through the clouds, brightening the day. Tonight, they had their standing Friday night gig. He needed to refocus his mind. Music came first. His faltering identity would have to wait for its turn another time. He tucked his phone away and reluctantly finished his last 3 hours.

The rain started around 8 pm. It was going to keep people from heading downtown for the evening. Lucas couldn't disagree with people wanting to stay home curled up on their warm sofa with a loved one, watching television instead. He craved a night like that.

"Check. Check. Test. Test." Then the first line of a song on repeat.

Two thumbs up from the guy they'd hired to do sound tonight. They'd decided to spend fifty dollars for every gig at that particular venue to employ someone.

Less hassles. Less stress.

They all left the stage and piled into an empty table next to the stage. The staff at the pub tried their best to keep it open for them. The band had given themselves extra time and had already consumed a huge amount of food and were working on their third drink each.

Lucas stopped talking, lowered his glass, and stared toward the door.

He swallowed.

Standing inside the entrance to the pub—Nick.

It was as though time stood still as he watched him. Nothing else mattered.

Just Nick.

I don't want to be gay.

Nick walked toward them with a fabulous, heartfelt smile

on his face. He clapped Mike on the back. "Thought I'd catch you guys tonight. Looking forward to playing with you all tomorrow night." They'd finalized the arrangements. Nick would be playing with them tomorrow night at Deckers. It made sense that he'd want to drop in tonight.

"Lucas." Nick nodded at him. "I've cleaned up those tracks a bit more. I'll send them to you."

"Yeah, okay … thanks." Lucas couldn't take his eyes off Nick. Everything about the guy turned him on. His eyes. His lips. His broad shoulders. The way he swept his hand through his hair. It was a visceral reaction to being around him. There was no way he could shut it off.

Jeezus.

His cock was getting hard beneath the table.

He could feel Nick's hand wrapped around it, stroking— tugging.

I don't want to be gay.

"I need to run to the washroom." Lucas struggled out past Samuel and headed for the stairs to the bathrooms. He thundered down them, ran into a stall, and slammed the door shut.

He just needed a minute to collect himself.

He couldn't be popping an erection on stage.

"Lucas?" He knew that voice. "Are you all right?"

"Go away, Nick."

I don't want to be gay.

"Are you sick? Can I get you something?"

"I'm feeling queasy." Lucas pulled a length of toilet paper off the roll and dabbed his sweaty forehead. "I might ask you to sub in for me. You said you know all our songs."

If Nick was on the stage, he could take off home and avoid his growing arousal. Being on stage while Nick watched him was not going to work for him.

I don't want to be gay.

"That's ridiculous. I'm not subbing for you." Nick knocked on the door. "Let me in."

"Please leave me alone."

"You looked like you were having fun until you spotted me. What's going on?"

It was going to make things worse, but deep inside, he wanted to feel the full effect of seeing Nick up close. To be breathing in the same space with him again.

Lucas unlocked and opened the stall door.

Nick pushed his way inside and closed the door behind him. "What's going on?"

I don't want to be gay.

Lucas shuddered. He was nearly in tears. He sat down on the toilet seat, elbows on his knees, and lowered his head into his hands. "I'm so confused."

"About what?"

Lucas looked up at Nick. "You. I'm confused about you."

Nick smiled. "Don't know why. I'm a pretty basic guy."

"You know that's not what I mean."

Nick lay his hand on Lucas' shoulder. "What can I do to help?"

Lucas rose to his feet. He crowded Nick against the stall door. "You can kiss me again." His reaction to Nick's lips would decide everything. His reaction had to be emotional. Not just sexual.

Nick cupped Lucas' face in both hands. "That I can do."

The kiss was sweet and slow. Lucas immersed himself in it—all of it. He searched every corner of it. His body was off and running. His cock was hard. But layered on top of the desire was a thick ribbon of emotional response. He wanted to be closer to Nick—not just his body—him. This wasn't just sexual. This wasn't just physical arousal.

I don't want to be gay.

Lucas pulled away but kept his hairline pressed to Nick's. The top of Nick's glasses pressed into the bridge of Lucas' nose. "I think I might be gay," he whispered.

"Is this the first time you've considered that?"

"I've been straight my whole damned life."

"And now you might have figured out you're not. What does that change?"

"Jeezus, Nick ... everything." Like absolutely everything. His entire existence was being turned on its head. What else didn't he know about himself?

"Are you freaking out a little?"

"You have no idea."

Nick wrapped his arms around Lucas and held him. "I'm here for you."

"I want you to be ... *here* for me." It was the subtlest hint he could drop. He'd never been comfortable with asking for what he wanted. It seemed for most of his life, he'd been asking for the wrong thing. This man—right now—the one holding him. He wanted him.

"Does that mean you'd like to try something different ... with me?" Nick asked.

Lucas shifted the angle of his head so he could see Nick's eyes. There was comfort in them. The type of comfort he'd been craving from every partner he'd ever been with.

"With you, I would."

Nick brushed the back of Lucas' head with his hand. "Then let's take this slow." He kissed Lucas—quick but sweet. "Are you going to be able to get up on stage? It's almost time."

Lucas nodded. He just needed to pull it together. He felt

better now that he'd told Nick he was seriously questioning his sexual identity. And that he wanted to try something non-platonic with Nick. He needed to know. He needed to know if he was gay.

If Nick was willing to put up with him and let him explore his sexuality at his own pace, he could keep his focus on the music for the night.

Chapter Four | Nick

Nick followed Lucas back up the stairs to the pub's main floor. What had transpired in the bathroom had surprised him. He had been sure Lucas would remain firmly rooted in denial.

I think I might be gay.

Lucas had said it aloud to him. The scowling, angry man had exposed a soft part of his heart. The desire to explore his most intimate yearnings with him. He'd treat that heart with great care.

Lucas wants to be with me.

Nick smiled as he sat down at the table with the other band members. They were chatting and laughing like a close-knit family. He'd heard they'd been together for 7 years.

That was quite the accomplishment for a cover band. He looked across the table at Lucas. He seemed more relaxed. The smallest of smiles turned up one side of Lucas' lips as he joined in on the conversation. Mike rose from his chair. "Let's get this show on the road."

They all hoisted themselves onto the stage. It was a big step up which required helping hands. As Nick took a sip of his beer, two women joined him at his table. They had to be the wives or girlfriends of the drummer and bass guitar player. Lucas' girlfriend would have been part of their troupe. They made quick introductions to him but then huddled amongst themselves, laughing and drinking. They were barely paying attention to the band. And certainly not to him.

Nick settled back in his chair and grinned as he watched

Lucas perform. Totally different guy. The guy on stage was radiant, charming, and jubilant—a perfect frontman and showman.

He wanted to bring *that* Lucas out to play.

And he was willing to pull out pick axes and spelunking gear to do it.

Lucas rocked back and forth to the music, strumming and singing. He was a natural. He belonged on the stage. He was the kind of guy who should have been discovered by now.

Maybe he could tour if he got an originals band together. Increase his chances.

Nick smirked. Of course, it was possible, he was biased.

He decided to stay for all three sets. On the last break, the band talked about going for a curry after they were done for the night. They'd invited him to join them.

It was a longer walk than if they had gone to a downtown pub. The restaurant was down some stairs in a shady part of town with homeless people crowding the doorways. The smell of curry infiltrated his sensations as they stepped through the door. He hadn't realized how hungry he was.

They found a table for four and flipped through the menu. They all decided on butter chicken. It was on their table with a time limit of thirty minutes to eat before the restaurant closed at 2 am.

Lucas had chosen a chair at a right angle to his. Nick read all sorts of things into that. Lucas could have easily taken the chair across from him. Maybe he was serious about trying with him.

In the bathroom, he hadn't been sure it wasn't just Lucas' fear talking. If he just needed a sounding board to bounce his possible gayness off. That he was afraid to be alone.

Nick was a little stunned when Lucas pressed his knee to

Nick's under the table. He could feel the heat of desire grow as their legs remained in contact.

His cock paid attention to the proximity. He hoped to hell he wouldn't have to use the washroom. His cock was swelling more by the second.

Nick took a chance and reached beneath the table and set his hand on Lucas' leg. He used his fingers to caress his thigh. If experience was anything to judge by, Lucas wouldn't be getting up anytime soon either. Lucas set his hand on top of Nick's and gripped it.

Now Nick could feel his heart beating loudly in his ears.

Lucas was taking huge strides.

Then as quick as the moment had happened, Lucas pulled away all contact. Nick searched Lucas' profile expression. Was he afraid of getting caught? Or had he changed his mind about them? Nick leaned toward him. "You all right?" he whispered.

"A bit anxious."

"Okay." Nick refocused on his food and finished the plate. Anxious was better than an *I don't want to do this*. They could work through anxious.

"We're closing in 5 minutes," their server said to them. "I need to settle your bills."

"I'll cover both our bills." Nick pointed at Lucas. "I owe him one."

"Thanks," Lucas grunted; the grumpy, agitated expression had returned. Nick wondered what had set it off. Two seconds ago Lucas had been begrudgingly animated while he talked.

They climbed the stairs back onto the street.

Mike pointed down the road. "Samuel and I are this way."

"I'm in the parking garage on Yates," Nick said.

"Me too," Lucas replied.

"Okay, see you guys tomorrow night." Nick flashed them

his biggest smile. He was excited about playing with them tomorrow night. His first time with them and it was a Saturday in one of the busiest pubs in Victoria. Mike must have liked what he heard when he was busking.

He and Lucas walked in silence for a couple of blocks.

"Do you want to practice with me tomorrow afternoon?" Lucas asked.

Nick bit his bottom lip. Was that an invitation to practice or something else? Lucas knew he didn't need to practice with him. The songs and vocal harmony were pretty simple.

"Are you asking me over to your place?" Nick asked.

Lucas stopped walking and turned to face him. Wow, seriously broody and anxious face. There were creases all over it. Even his mouth was turned down. Lucas was at odds.

"I'm not looking for anything to happen," Lucas said.

"Then it won't." Unless their passion overwhelmed them and they found themselves in the bedroom. In that case, Nick would do everything to ensure it was special for Lucas.

Lucas stepped toward Nick and cupped his face in one hand. The other grabbed the front of Nick's coat. Lucas pulled Nick forward into a kiss. A kiss that took Nick's breath away.

There was so much ravenous need there.

Nick felt a little dizzy as they walked the rest of the distance to the parking garage. Nick followed Lucas to his truck. He pressed Lucas' back against his driver's door.

"One more kiss before we part ways," Nick said.

Lucas' mouth was receptive—yearning. Their tongues fought for dominance. Nick leaned against Lucas and pressed his hard, jeans-bound cock to Lucas'. Lucas gripped him tighter. Nick rocked his hips as he continued his assault on Lucas' lips. Grinding—sighing—moaning.

The only thing that stopped them … a group of people

walking past in search of their car. Nick gave Lucas one last kiss and stepped back so Lucas could open his door.

"We can finish that tomorrow if you want," Nick said.

It seemed Lucas had been rendered speechless. He just nodded and climbed into his truck. Some of the creases had left Lucas' face. After Lucas pulled out of the spot, he waved at Nick.

It was an adorable, nervous wave with so much uncertainty in his eyes. It made Nick feel uneasy. This would be the first time he had dated someone with less experience than him.

He hoped he didn't fuck it up.

It was a nice older house. Good neighborhood. He'd always liked Oak Bay. The rent there must be astronomical, though. That's why he shared a house with three other guys in Esquimalt.

Nick knocked on the door and waited. It took Lucas a while to finally open it. He was wearing grey sweatpants and a form-fitting white t-shirt. He was dressed to play. And not with music.

His gaze wandered up and down Lucas.

Jeezus Christ.

Lucas was going commando. His cock was already at half-mast. He could see the clear outline of Lucas' cockhead beneath the fabric.

"I thought you'd never get here," Lucas said.

Nick swept into the front entry and Lucas closed the door. Nick didn't even have his coat off when Lucas sealed their lips together. The kiss was hungry and aggressive. His whole body was buzzing with lust by the time Lucas pulled away. He objected to being separated with a soft moan.

"Let's go to the living room," Lucas said.

Nick shrugged off his coat onto the floor and chased after Lucas. The living room was relaxed and homey as though someone could spend a lot of time in there reading a book and drinking tea. He wondered who had decorated it. Was it Lucas or his ex-girlfriend?

Lucas sat on the sofa with his arms out. Nick took that as an invitation and climbed onto the sofa and straddled Lucas's hips. He cupped Lucas' face and kissed him.

They became lost in each other.

They went from sitting on the sofa to Lucas being layered on top of Nick in mere seconds. Lucas wasn't messing around. Nick spread his legs to accommodate him; their hard cocks trapped between them. Nick gripped onto Lucas' ass and guided him to thrust against him.

He lifted his head as Lucas nudged it aside and started sucking on and kissing his neck. Nick groaned and lifted his hands onto the back of Lucas' neck. He didn't want him to stop.

Thrusting—and sucking.

And using his teeth to excite his skin.

Nick regretted wearing jeans. The pressure beneath his fly was intense but that problem was soon solved. Lucas shimmied down Nick's body, undid Nick's pants, and hauled them off his hips.

His weeping cock was exposed to the air.

I thought we were taking it slow.

"I thought we were taking it slow?"

Lucas looked up at him. "I've been jerking off to the thought of you all morning. I need the real thing. I need to touch you." With that said Lucas wrapped his fingers around Nick's cock.

Nick wasn't about to object. He'd promised Lucas to take it slow but that speed was something to be dictated by Lucas. If that speed included a handjob, he wasn't going to argue.

Lucas shuffled further down the sofa.

Oh, my god.

Nick pitched his head back, his chest rising off the sofa—his hips bucked up as Lucas sucked his cockhead into his mouth.

Fuck.

From heterosexual to sucking cock in two seconds flat.

He dug his hands into Lucas' hair and rode the rhythm of Lucas' swallowing and retreating on and off his cock as though Lucas had been designed to suck dick.

Lucas supported himself with his elbow on one of Nick's hips and reached down into his own pants with the other hand. Nick could feel the groan from Lucas' throat right through his cock.

Within moments, Lucas stopped sucking and shuddered and grunted. His body convulsed over and over again as he released the latest pressure he'd been dealing with all day.

Lucas drew his hand out of his pants and used it to jack Nick's cock. Lucas' fingers had splatters of his cum on them. He smeared the slickness up and down Nick's shaft.

That very act of coating Nick's cock with his own cum almost made Nick blow his load.

Then Lucas dove back on with his mouth.

Oh, god ... right there.

Lucas' tongue was divine, licking and swirling, creating a euphoric trip of escalating desperation. Nick was close. He reminded himself that it was Lucas' first time. He guided Lucas' mouth away from his cock, touched himself, stroking fast, and came hard onto his stomach.

Lucas looked disappointed.

"Not on your first time," Nick said. "You think you want it

but it can be a bit shocking."

"Next time," Lucas said. "I want it next time."

"Okay. Next time." Nick held out his arms and Lucas crawled up his body and landed on his chest. Lucas tucked his hot breath against the skin behind Nick's ear.

Nick wrapped Lucas up in his arms. "This is the best part."

"What about the other part? I thought I did pretty good. You seemed to like it."

"You're a natural."

"I've been given a lot of blowjobs. I know what works."

"I'll be sure to thank all your previous girlfriends." Nick laughed and brushed his hand through the semi-long strands of Lucas' hair. "I didn't think you'd be ready for that."

"Me either." Lucas kissed Nick's neck. "But you've been haunting my thoughts. I've been craving things I never thought I would. I actually want to be physical with you."

"That's different than it's been in the past?"

"Confession." Lucas rose on one arm so he could look Nick in the eyes. "I hated having sex with my girlfriend. I've hated having sex with every woman I've ever been with. Other than in high school when my hormones were in overdrive and I would screw anything."

"You never thought about experimenting?"

"In university, a guy kissed me. It messed with my head, he made me so hard."

"You didn't pursue him?"

Lucas smiled a little. Actually bloody smiled. "He was kind of a drive-by kiss."

"And yet you pressed on with women."

"I was convinced I was straight. Possibly asexual."

"That's just the sexual component of a committed relationship. How was your emotional relationship with your girlfriend?" There were things he needed to know about Lucas before they proceeded any further. He'd planned on leaving it for another time but Lucas had advanced their relationship faster than he'd mapped out in his head. There could be stumbling blocks.

Lucas closed his eyes and breathed in and out a few times.

"There was nothing there. Like *nothing*. I didn't even love her as a friend."

Wow. Okay.

"Why on earth did you stay with her?"

"Like I told you before, I didn't want to be alone."

"Is that why you're jumping in so hard with me?" That was an important question. He didn't want to be added to a long string of Lucas' failed relationships.

Lucas furrowed his brow. "I would never do that to you—use you like that."

Nick stroked Lucas' cheek. "Why not?"

"I have too much respect for you."

"And you didn't have respect for your girlfriend?" Nick knew he was being harsh but Lucas needed to figure out where he had gone wrong in the past before they moved forward.

Lucas shoved himself off the sofa.

"I think I want to be alone now."

Nick redressed his lower half. "I get it. You have some things you need to think about." He joined Lucas in the middle of the living room. "Think about what I asked." He leaned in and gave Lucas a quick kiss on the lips. "I'll be waiting for you when you come out the other side."

Saturday night started a little awkward. Lucas refused to acknowledge him. Which wasn't going to work when they started the show. There needed to be communication between them.

Nick finished tuning his guitar, then the band did a quick sound check. There was no dedicated reserved table for them, so after the sound check, they ended up crowded against the bar.

Not only was Lucas refusing to acknowledge him, but Lucas hadn't answered the solitary text Nick had sent him a couple of hours after he'd left Lucas'.

Do you need to talk?

He might have pissed Lucas off enough to make him walk. While they were waiting for their first set to start, Lucas just stared into his beer, glowering at it.

Even on stage, Lucas was off his game. The audience probably didn't notice but he was acting more reserved than he had the night before.

During their second break, Nick headed outside for some fresh air. Even on a cold April night, the crowds of people inside were heating up the place.

He didn't realize Lucas had followed him until he turned and leaned against the front of the building so he could have a view of the ocean.

Instead, he had a view of Lucas.

"I respected her as a woman," Lucas said. "It didn't extend further than that."

"That's harsh. Can you come to terms with that?"

Lucas shook his head. "I don't know if I can do that. It wasn't fair on her."

"She's a grown woman. She had plenty of opportunities to end it."

Lucas hung his head low. "I don't like to think we were using each other all that time."

"I think it was your way of staying buried in the closet."

Lucas looked up at him. "I'm still in there."

"But you want to keep seeing me, right?"

"Not going to lie. I was a bit ticked off with you this afternoon for making me dig. It brought up a lot of stuff." Lucas reached for Nick's hand and touched his fingers. "I forgave you."

"How much did you forgive me?" Nick smiled and tugged on Lucas' coat.

"Guys, it's time!" Mike shouted from the doors. "You sticking around, Nick?"

"Not sure yet!" Mike wandered back inside. Nick smiled at Lucas. "Am I sticking around until the end of the last set?"

"I'd like you to."

"And then what?"

"And then I still need some time to think."

Nick brushed his hand through his hair. Lucas' enthusiasm had faded. He might have been making room in that closet to climb further into it. "You're not sure you want to date me."

"I just need time."

Those were never good words coming from a potential partner. That usually ended in a *No, I've decided against it*. He didn't say another word. He'd give Lucas his time.

What else could he do?

Chapter Five | Lucas

It was difficult to concentrate on the guitar chords and lyrics. Never mind sing them properly. Lucas' heart wasn't in it. For the first time in his life, he wanted off the stage early.

Nick had challenged him to analyze his relationship with Angie. He understood why. Nick didn't want him falling into the same trap again. Getting into a relationship to combat loneliness.

They finished their last song and the crowd on the dance floor cheered. Some people started chanting *one more song*. Normally, they would have played another. But Lucas didn't have it in him. He didn't direct the band to play anything else to finish out the night.

"You all right?" Samuel clapped a hand on Lucas' shoulder. "You missing Angie?"

Lucas frowned. "No. We were long destined for that breakup."

"Too soon to start dating again, I guess."

Lucas so badly wanted to tell Samuel he was considering changing things up. Dating a guy this time. See how it went. Maybe he'd find the connection he'd been seeking … with a man.

Instead, he just emitted a, "Yup."

Lucas picked up a cable and coiled it in loops to store it away. There were cables scattered all over the stage. Everyone was pitching in to tear down.

Even Nick.

Lucas watched him for a few moments. He wanted to touch him again. The way he had touched him this afternoon. He'd been surprised at how good Nick's cock felt in his mouth.

Then the fear crept in.

I don't want to be gay.

Those words had been playing on repeat since he had cum all over himself while sucking another guy's cock. And how much that heavy shaft on his tongue had turned him on.

Maybe he could become a loner.

Then he wouldn't have to worry about whether he was gay.

I don't want to be gay.

Those words kept flashing like a neon sign in his mind.

What would it mean if he was gay? Would it change anything? Would his bandmates look at him differently? Would it affect his career if he decided to pursue his own music? There were many reasons he didn't want to be gay. The prominent reason was it was foreign to him. It was foreign and it was frightening to think he was not in control of his body. That his body *and mind* wanted something different than what society expected.

Lucas wandered over to Nick.

"Can we talk?" he asked.

"Sure." Nick flashed Lucas one of his brilliant smiles. "We can head out to the smoke pit. It's a bit more protected from the wind back there as long as you don't mind a bit of cigarette smoke."

"I used to smoke. I'm good with it."

"How long were you a smoker?" Nick asked as they made their way outside.

"Nine years. Angie made me quit."

"Bonus points for Angie."

"Yeah, it wasn't all bad with her."

They settled in a corner, leaning against some wooden fencing.

"I'm trying to sort through something," Lucas said. "If I'm gay, I would have been jonesing for guys over the years, right?"

Nick shook his head. "Not necessarily. I don't like every guy I see. Straight people don't like every person of the opposite sex they see. Being attracted to someone is quite rare."

"I think *rare* is a bit of an exaggeration."

"Yeah, okay. But it doesn't happen a lot … not that real, life partner kind of attraction." Nick brushed his fingers down Lucas' sleeve. "Were you attracted to the women you dated?"

Lucas shook his head. "No. Maybe one or two. Not heavily, though."

"What about me?"

Wow.

Wasn't that obvious? They'd had some intense make-out sessions and he'd given Nick a blowjob that afternoon. But did he dare expose the extent to which Nick was ticking all of his boxes? Charming. Intelligent. Joyous. Caring. Warm. And fucking gorgeous.

It would be quite the admission to answer him fully and truthfully. Was he attracted to him? God, yes. But he still wasn't sure if he wanted to date Nick. If he did date him, he'd be jumping squarely into the gay category. He hadn't decided if he wanted to do that.

He watched the news. He knew how hard it was for gay people to even exist. Never mind having all the same rights as straight people and having even a modicum of respect from them.

There would be countries he would have to avoid if he had a gay partner. They'd always be on the lookout for trouble. They might face discrimination even within Canada.

He looked at Nick.

Maybe he was worth it. If he listened to his head, he might never find happiness. If he listened to his heart, he might find love. Maybe it was time to step off the ledge into the unknown.

Lucas stepped closer to Nick and placed a hand on his chest.

"Yes, I'm definitely attracted to you. And I need you to kiss me."

Nick looked around. "Here? In front of everyone?"

"I don't care about them. You're the only person that matters."

Lucas leaned into Nick's palm as Nick stroked his jaw. Nick wrapped his arm around Lucas' waist, tugged him close, and kissed him. Not a quick kiss. A slow, languishing one. One filled with meaning. Filled with longing. One containing a promise that Nick had his back.

Someone cleared their throat beside them.

They pulled apart.

"Hey, we're leaving now," Mike said. "You two staying behind for a bit?"

Lucas furrowed his brow as he looked at Mike. That was it? No surprise in his voice when he walked in on him and Nick kissing. Nothing? Just a *Hey, we're leaving now*?

I'm gay. And Mike doesn't give a shit.

"No, I think I'm going to Nick's tonight."

Nick smiled at Lucas. The kind of smile that would bring gay men to their knees. Nick's presence was space occupying; vast. He lit up every corner of a room with his existence.

"Yeah," Nick said, then laughed. "We're going to play video games."

Mike snorted out a laugh. "Whatever you want to call it. None of my business." He patted Nick on the shoulder. "Glad you're both happy, though. Maybe you'll be able to cheer Lucas up."

"Challenge accepted." Followed by a goofy grin on Nick's face. Mike left and Nick's gaze fell on Lucas. He caught his attention. "Are you sure about this? Coming back to my place?"

No, he wasn't sure. Lucas knew he needed to be near Nick. To be wrapped up in his arms. To be told everything was going to be okay. To feel Nick's naked body against his.

Lucas leaned in and kissed Nick's neck.

"I want you so bad," he whispered.

Nick cleared his throat. "Then I suggest we get out of here."

They took Lucas' truck. Ten minutes later, they pulled into Nick's driveway. The walk to the front door was in silence. Like something sacred was about to happen.

Two of the guys were up, drunk, and playing video games in the living room. Lucas knew both of them. He'd even played a duo with one of them last month.

"Oh, hey, Lucas." The guy he'd played with, Benjamin, jumped to his feet and approached them. He reached out his hand and Lucas shook it.

"Benjamin. How's it going?"

"Busy. Lots of gigs. Tonight was a fluke having the night off."

"Yeah, we've been busy too."

Benjamin looked at Nick, then back at Lucas.

"So, what are you doing here? Working on some music with Nick?"

Nick stepped in. "Something like that." He ran his hand up Lucas' back from his ass to the base of Lucas' neck where he gripped it. He left his hand there, clearly visible to Benjamin.

"Oh." Benjamin stepped back. "Sorry. I had no idea,

Lucas."

"We just met recently," Lucas said as though that might explain anything.

Benjamin made a dismissive move with one hand. "Yeah, yeah. Whatever. Not my business." He flopped back on the sofa and picked up his game controller. He went right back to hollering at his opponent as he drove his race car down a track. Not even a second glance.

Nick led Lucas down a hallway and into his bedroom. He shut and locked the door behind them. "See. No big deal. So far, nobody cares."

"Maybe we should have gone back to my place. I don't live with anyone."

"Next time." Nick pushed Lucas backward and trapped him against the door. "Because, I promise you, you are going to want a next time."

Lucas smirked. "You're awfully confident."

"I just have a feeling." Nick kissed Lucas and ran his hands up under Lucas' shirt. His hands were cold. The exploring fingertips lit up all the little nerve endings on his back.

His cock started to ache.

Nick dragged Lucas' bottom lip down with his teeth and released it.

"I have a feeling," he reiterated, "that you and I are going to be very compatible."

He stepped away from Lucas, walked across the room to his dresser, took off his glasses, and placed them on the surface along with a few other pairs. He loved Nick with his glasses off. You could see his stunning eyes and thick lashes better.

Lucas soaked in the sight of him and then looked around the room. It was tidy. A bright checkered bedcover dominated the room. That and all the musical equipment. Electric guitars, bass guitars. Even a keyboard.

"You play keyboards?" Lucas asked.

"I've picked up a bit over the years. I'm not too bad on the drums either."

"Talented." Lucas shrugged out of his coat. There was a hook on the back of the door. He hung his fleece-lined jean jacket there. Soon joined by Nick's heavy sweater coat.

"I like to play around with different instruments." Nick grabbed the bottom of his shirt and peeled it off over his head. He tossed it to one side. "Amongst other things."

Lucas moved closer to him. He lifted one hand and stroked Nick's chest. It was smooth and firm. A muscular and tantalizing terrain of ripples. A strip of dark hair descended from his belly button to the top of his pants. He wanted to be reacquainted with where that trail led.

He brushed his hand back across Nick's chest. Nick sucked in a breath as Lucas' hand rubbed across his hard, taut nipple. He'd be starting there. He flicked Nick's nipple with the tip of his tongue, then sucked it into his mouth. It felt firm and perfect. Nick groaned and jammed his hand into Lucas' hair. Lucas kissed his way across to the other dark pink nub. It was exquisite in its simplicity; the feel of it beneath his lips and the way Nick responded when he played with it.

Lucas slowly sunk to his knees, kissing Nick's skin the whole way down. He licked the trail of soft hair that disappeared behind the band of Nick's jeans, then slowly cupped Nick's jeans-covered cock with his mouth. Kissing, licking, mouthing, running his teeth across it.

"Fuck," Nick exhaled and set his hand on Lucas' head.

With anxious fingers, Lucas undid the button and fly on Nick's pants. Nick helped him to shimmy his jeans and underwear off his hips. And then it was right there. The length and weight he'd been craving since the afternoon. Lucas was quick to take it into his mouth.

Holding the base of Nick's cock and using his hand to stroke it when he needed to catch his breath, he sucked Nick until his cock was hot and tight.

Nick touched the bottom of Lucas' chin, directing him to stand. The kiss that followed was like someone on the verge of insanity. Lucas had never felt as desired. Nick was desperate for him.

"Too many clothes," Nick panted when they parted.

Lucas stripped faster than he'd ever done before. Nick stepped out of the jeans and underwear pooled around his ankles and pushed Lucas toward the bed. Nick stripped off his socks as Lucas climbed onto the mattress, laid down, and found a pillow to put beneath his head.

This was monumental, lying in a guy's bed, prepared to have sex with him. Before Nick, it had been a fantasy. It wasn't until he met Nick that he thought his fantasy might come true.

He watched Nick make a trip to the bedside table before he joined Lucas on the bed. He had a bottle of lube and a couple of foil-wrapped condoms in his hand.

Lucas couldn't take his eyes off what was being brought to the bed. A rush of desire swept through his body. He was so ready for this. He wanted Nick all over and inside him.

Nick set the supplies aside and straddled Lucas' hips. He leaned forward enough that their hard cocks pressed together. He kissed Lucas—long and slow.

Nick's eyes were hooded when he withdrew as though he'd overindulged with drink. "You undo me, Lucas," he whispered. "I can't get enough of you."

"Take as much as you want." Lucas put his hands over his head. He meant it. There was no part of himself that he wanted to keep from Nick. He could have it all.

Nick drifted down Lucas' body. Kissing his chest—his abs—the base of his cock. Lucas gasped and closed his eyes as Nick sucked his cock into his mouth. It was a habit—closing his eyes. He didn't want to be in the dark. He opened his eyes and watched Nick between his legs.

Fuck.

Nick was beautiful down there. He couldn't look away. Nick stretched his arm up and placed one hand on Lucas' chest. Lucas set his hand on Nick's. Nick intertwined their fingers.

Every bit of saliva and suction nearly brought Lucas to tears. This was a feeling he'd been seeking his entire adult life. Someone who was meant to be down there giving him incredible pleasure. Not the countless women who hadn't elicited this response from him.

Nick sucked hard, then let Lucas' cock slip from his mouth. He reached for the bottle of lube. Lucas tracked Nick's movements. Nick nudged Lucas to open his legs.

Without a second of hesitation, Lucas brought his feet up and placed them on the bed near his ass, and dropped his legs open. Nick coated his fingers in lube, then took Lucas' cock back into his mouth. As Nick sucked his cock, one of Nick's fingers circled Lucas' hole.

Lucas groaned and ground his ass into the bedding.

He wanted it.

As Nick's finger slid into his hole, Lucas felt as though his lashes might permanently flutter right off. His groan was more guttural this time. It was carnal—primal.

Nick moved his mouth from Lucas' cock to his balls, sucking on one and then the other as he slid a second finger into Lucas' hole. Nick bent his fingers and swept them across a sensitive area deep inside that made Lucas' whole body light up.

"Oh, Nick …."

Nick kissed the inside of his thigh and added a third finger. The addition made Lucas want to bear down. The craving and desperation to be filled was intense and—life-changing.

Lucas gasped and grunted as Nick rocked his fingers in and out of his hole.

"Enough, Nick." Lucas touched Nick's hand. "I need you."

"I'm here for you." Nick's fingers slipped from Lucas' hole and he was back on Lucas' lips. The pressure and emotion behind each kiss were heart-stopping. Nick sat back, ripped open a condom wrapper with his teeth, tossed it aside, and rolled the condom onto his cock.

Then Nick was back. They took a moment to stare into each other's eyes. Lucas wrapped his arms around Nick. He felt safe with him. Nick caressed Lucas' lips with his. The emotion behind the kiss made Lucas a promise that Nick would take special care of him.

It was the most cherished Lucas had ever felt in his life.

Lucas moaned and clutched Nick's shoulders tightly as Nick's cockhead breached his hole. He exhaled and relaxed. Nick took his mouth again and encouraged a dance with their tongues to distract him. Nick sunk his cock in a little further. Lucas whined. The burn was incredible.

"You're all right," Nick whispered.

Lucas mewled hard and loud as Nick closed the distance between them. Nick was seated all the way inside him. Lucas could feel Nick's cock in his belly. He needed to adjust to being filled.

"Give me a second," Lucas said.

"As long as you need."

Nick dropped gentle kisses all over Lucas' face. His

eyebrows. Eyelids. Nose. Cheeks. Chin. Then to his lips. Lucas hummed and chased Nick's mouth. Nick shifted his hips back.

The dragging sensation as Nick's cock withdrew was unwelcome.

"Come back to me," Lucas whimpered.

Nick thrust slow and high into Lucas. A whole new universe opened up. Lucas rolled his eyes back and savored every sensation. The heat building between them. The sound of Nick breathing—groaning. The scent of fresh laundry. The feel of Nick's cock buried deep inside him.

Nick pumped his hips with gentle, loving strokes; each time he withdrew completely, then thrust as high as he could go inside Lucas on the return.

Bliss.

It's the only word to describe what Lucas was feeling. Being in the arms of a man as he caressed him deep inside for the first time was an experience he'd cherish forever.

He reached for his cock. It had recovered after the initial shock from the pain. Now it was rock hard and weeping long strings of precum onto his belly.

When he started stroking it, Nick increased his pace. Sparks—serious fucking sparks erupted behind his eyes as Nick hammered into him.

Lucas grunted, wrapped his hand behind one knee, and lifted his leg. He wanted every inch of Nick's cock pounding into him.

Nick received the message and began thrusting harder and faster into Lucas. The force jostled every muscle in Lucas' body. He grunted and groaned, and called Nick's name.

The room filled with *Fuck* and *Oh, my God—and Harder.*

A sweat broke out on Nick's brow and his chest. The heat between them was incredible. There was no way the guys downstairs couldn't hear them. Lucas didn't care.

All sorts of loud guttural sounds were coming out of him.

He'd never been this hard, this desperate—this enraptured. He kept pumping his cock. Nick changed his angle and dragged across his gland a few times. The added sensation drove him over the edge. He came in chest-covering spurts and drops.

Nick sat back, lifted both of Lucas' legs onto his shoulders, and drilled hard into him. Lucas watched Nick's face. It was cycling through cascades of pleasure. His mouth was open, panting.

Nick looked down at Lucas. Caught him staring, and gave him a wide smile.

Then Nick closed his eyes and he was summiting again. A droplet of sweat ran down the bridge of Nick's nose and hung poised at the tip. A few thrusts later it landed on Lucas' chest.

The sound of Nick grunting filled the room. It was an entirely male sound. Lucas closed his eyes and enjoyed the soundtrack and the feeling of Nick pumping his cock into his belly.

Nick's cock jumped inside him.

This was the moment.

Nick jerked, swore, and his body went rigid buried deep inside. Then he pumped slowly as he milked his cock into the condom in Lucas' ass. Nick released Lucas' legs and lowered his sweat-slicked chest onto Lucas'. Lucas was aware of the fact Nick had just laid his chest on his cum.

Nick gave him a sweet kiss. It was as if they were checking in with each other. Lucas was hungry for Nick's lips. He met every one of Nick's kisses with one of his own.

Nick ended the tender moment with a final kiss, then pulled away and looked down into Lucas' eyes. "You all right?"

"Better than all right. Reality gave me a serious smack across the face."

Nick grinned. "Oh, yeah?"

Lucas couldn't stop a smile from stretching across his face. "I am *so* gay."

"Well." Nick rolled off Lucas, peeled off his condom, tied a knot in it, dropped it onto the floor, and rolled back to face Lucas. "I'm happy you finally accepted yourself." He stroked Lucas' face. "Because I think you're pretty incredible."

Lucas threw an arm over his eyes. "No, *you* were incredible. I just had to lay there."

"You want to top sometimes?"

Lucas lowered his arm. He hadn't thought guys would take turns. It was hetero thinking, he knew that. The *man* always topped unless the straight couple was into pegging.

"You'd be into that?"

"Yeah, I'm vers. I need a good fucking sometimes."

Fucking.

Is that what they were doing? It sounded so crude for an experience that had brought him so much joy. Nick threw his arm over Lucas' chest and his leg over Lucas' thighs.

A shiver of desire rippled through Lucas as Nick kissed the side of his neck.

He'd be ready to go again after Nick rested for a while. He decided he'd be staying over. He had no intention of climbing out of Nick's warm, fragrant bed.

Maybe a shower. They were coated in sweat and cum.

Lucas sighed and embraced Nick. By the sound of his breathing, he was nearly asleep already. Lucas soon joined him there. They both awoke while it was still dark. Correction. Lucas kissed Nick's forehead until he woke up. Lucas was met with a huge smile and a quick kiss.

The second time he was filled by Nick's cock wasn't as painful. His ass was still primed. The third time, no pain at all. Just pure ecstasy. They fell asleep, exhausted, and didn't stir until the sun streamed in through the curtains. Nick woke Lucas up with his mouth around Lucas' cock.

Lucas stretched and enjoyed the morning gift. Nick sucked him until he came down Nick's throat. Then Nick licked him clean and suggested they get organized for breakfast.

Chapter Six | Nick

The toast popped from the toaster. Nick grabbed it quickly so he wouldn't burn his fingers, and threw the slices onto a plate. Lucas was taking care of some bacon and eggs.

Nick buttered the toast and retrieved eggs from the fridge. Luke set pieces of bacon on a sheet of paper towel. He cracked four eggs into the bacon grease.

They'd showered before they came down to the kitchen. They'd washed and shampooed each other and explored each other's bodies. They'd left their cocks alone. They were both sore.

One of Nick's roommates wandered into the kitchen. The one Lucas had spoken to—Benjamin. He went straight to the coffee pot. He looked exhausted.

"Rough night?" Nick asked Benjamin.

"Yeah." He turned to look at Nick. "If you're going to keep seeing Lucas, we are either going to have to soundproof your room or you need to go to his place."

"Sorry. Were we that loud?" Nick asked.

"I have your name being hollered playing on a loop in my head." Benjamin laughed and poured himself a huge cup of coffee. "Wish I had that much fun in bed with women."

Benjamin was still laughing when he left the kitchen.

Nick looked over at Luke. He was crimson red with embarrassment. Nick smiled at him. "Loosen up. Not a big deal." He stepped closer to Lucas and rubbed circles on his back. He could tell Lucas was mortified. "Those guys are just as bad when they have women over."

Lucas grunted and concentrated on the fried eggs. He

cooked them to perfection and lifted them onto the plates. They each snagged strips of bacon and went to sit at the table.

"Next time, we're meeting at my place," Lucas said.

"Oh, so I was right. You *do* want a next time."

Lucas scowled at his plate as he sopped up the yolk of the egg with his toast. Nick was still learning to decipher Lucas' facial expressions. This one, he knew. This one was Lucas thinking. Formulating his words. He'd be like this for a few seconds longer.

"I liked it," Lucas said at last. "A lot."

"I figured as much—since you wanted it three times last night."

Lucas turned his head and looked at Nick. "I want more than just sex with you."

"You're looking for more … as in a relationship?"

"Can we try that? Hang out more. Record music. Play music together. Get to know each other. I want to know you better, Nick. I want to know everything about you."

That was a lot of words all at once for Lucas. And they were heartfelt words, coming from a place Nick suspected rarely saw the light of day. Nick sighed. He didn't have a good track record. Would Lucas still be interested if he knew how disastrous his love life had been?

"I've never stayed with any one person for longer than a few months," Nick said. "Most of them have been women. Most of them haven't been musicians. Almost all of them never got me."

Lucas reached for Nick's hand. "I get you. I know how music takes up a huge part of your life. It's constantly in your head. How your fingers itch to get on a set of strings."

Nick accepted Lucas's hand. Lucas was right. They lived similar lives. Lucas understood the long hours of dedication.

The late nights. The constant networking meant even when you weren't playing yourself, you were out late most nights listening to other musicians.

None of the partners he'd been with had understood that. He slept until noon, then he was holed up in a room all afternoon practicing and writing songs. Then night would roll around and he'd be out the door just as his partner was getting home from work.

It was rare for them to see each other.

It would be different with Lucas. He would come with him on those nights he was playing or going out. He knew all the same people Nick would eventually know. Lucas' goals and dreams were practically in tandem with his. And the sex was amazing. Mind-blowing amazing.

There was a soft, gentle heart beating beneath all that outward angst. When they were having sex, Lucas exposed that part of himself. The second time they'd done it last night, Lucas had started crying. He'd said it was because he was so overwhelmed. It had made Nick tear up.

The kiss after that exchange had been significant. They were bonding in ways Nick never had before with anyone. Maybe Lucas was the one. The one he would love and cherish until his dying breath. That's what he wanted in his life. He was done with one-night stands.

At the age of thirty-five, he was looking to settle down.

Nick rose from his seat and stood behind Lucas, massaging his shoulders. He kissed the top of Lucas' head. "I only want to try that if you're serious about me. I don't want to be played."

Lucas twisted in his seat. "I would never play you." The look on Lucas's face was a mix of pleading and panic. There was no doubt that Lucas was serious.

"Should we go downstairs and lay down another few of

your tracks? Maybe add some layers onto the ones we've done already. Nice way to spend a Saturday with someone that gets you."

"Yeah, it is." Lucas joined Nick behind the chair, held his face, and kissed him. A delicious, slow, sultry kiss. They were making a promise to each other. That they were going to try to grow this relationship into something more. Nick was ready for it. With Lucas—he was ready.

The rest of the day passed and night fell. They hadn't even stopped to eat lunch, they were so wrapped up in what they were doing. Lucas' songs were starting to sound amazing. They'd replaced all the original tracks with crisper guitar lines, vocals, and harmonies that worked well.

They were listening to the final song they had worked on. It was release-ready. Lucas had spent an hour setting up an account on a music-streaming site. He would get paid for every listen of his song. It was a pittance but it would add up if the song became popular.

Nick prepared the file and sent it to his computer. He let Luke do the honors and upload the song file onto the streaming site. They would have to wait until it went live.

It should take an hour or so.

Lucas looked at his phone. "It's 6 already. Do you have a gig tonight?"

"Yeah, I'm subbing in for a lead guitarist tonight."

"Which band?"

Nick snorted out a laugh. "Death by Blackberries." He giggled at Lucas' expression. "What? It's good money. They're paying me $250 for jumping in at the last minute."

"They do *not* play soft rock."

"Luckily, I was in a metal band in Ottawa for a couple of years. The Blackberry guys play all the same stuff. Didn't take me long to refresh my memory."

Lucas actually smiled. "I have to see this. I'm not playing anywhere tonight. I am officially your date for the night. Not missing this for anything."

"A date, hey?"

"Or we could call it hanging out."

"No, I like *date*." Date implied they were growing their relationship. This wasn't just two guys hanging out, even though that's what it would feel like for the most part. Lucas was easy to be with. Conversation flowed between them. Their love of music alone brought them closer.

"What time are you playing?"

"At 9. Have to be there at 8 to set up."

Lucas smirked. "Yeah, I know the drill."

Nick leaned over and kissed Lucas. "And that is one of the things I like about you. I can talk about this band stuff and you've either experienced it or you're friends with someone who has. We're living in the same orbit. I think we were bound to collide eventually."

"As soon as I saw you, I knew." Lucas fiddled with his guitar strap. "All I saw at first was the back of you. Hadn't even seen your face yet."

Nick laughed. "You liked my ass?"

Lucas smirked. "I noticed your ass, but there was a deeper pull that was undeniable. Then I saw your face. You were so gorgeous. My heart just about beat out of my chest. I had to talk to you. I would've been sick if I hadn't collected the courage to seek you out."

"It was the sound of your voice that caught my attention. Even above the loud music, you have a warm tone in your voice. It comes out when you sing. It's smooth and sexy." Nick set his hand on Lucas' thigh. "Then our eyes met and I knew we would be drawn to each other again."

"That night when I saw you busking, I was so disappointed," Lucas said. "I was a little annoyed at Mike for asking you to play with us."

"Why did you invite me for cheesecake if you didn't approve of me?"

"Again that pull." Lucas crossed his arms. Nick suspected Luke was opening up more for him than he'd done for anyone before him. "I couldn't walk away. Not without talking to you first. It came on like a desperate need. And then the way you looked at me across the table ... I thought I might spontaneously ignite. I'd never wanted to be with someone that fiercely before. I didn't dare shake your hand again. I was afraid I would haul you into my arms and kiss you."

"I would have let you. I felt it too. I thought we were running the risk of ending up in a back alley somewhere with me fucking the daylights out of you."

Lucas cleared his throat. "I'm glad we didn't do that."

"Me too. Last night was perfect." Nick looked at his phone. "I need to go over a few songs with more complicated guitar solos. Can I meet you there?"

"Sure. Where are you playing?"

"Freemans."

Lucas snorted. "God. Taking our lives into our hands going down there."

"You're a strong, muscular guy. You'll be fine."

Lucas stepped over a multitude of wires as he made his way to the door that led to the stairs. "I'll be there at 8. I've heard their burgers aren't bad."

"Okay. See you then." Lucas landed a soft kiss on Nick's lips. Nick was going to remember the feeling of that kiss all night until he could get another one. And another—and another.

He hoped Lucas would invite him back to his place tonight. He wanted to fall asleep in Lucas' arms again. He wanted to make him cry out as loud as he wanted. They had been noisy last night, but he could sense Lucas was holding back. Nick wanted to unleash him.

Nick followed Lucas up to the door. They shared another kiss before Lucas walked to his truck and headed home. A hole the size of the Yukon opened up in Nick's chest.

They'd only be apart for a few hours but it was going to seem like a lifetime.

Playing with the Death by Blackberries metal band was a blast. It had been a long time since Nick had been able to scream, rip shrill licks from his guitar, and act like an idiot, dancing around. He was panting by the time they finished their first set.

If he'd known his acting like a fool on stage was the thing that would bring joy to Lucas' face, he would have done it sooner. Lucas had been clapping and laughing at his antics.

He wandered to the table Lucas was sitting at and dropped into a chair. Lucas had ordered him a beer near the end of his set. It was still cold. He gulped down half of it in one go.

He was parched.

He leaned sideways in his chair and gave Lucas a quick kiss. Lucas had made it quite clear that he wasn't averse to public displays of affection by kissing him in Decker's smoke pit.

The band wouldn't care. Two of the guys were bisexual too. They both had girlfriends but they had been with guys too. One of the guys had expressed that he was jealous. He enjoyed gay sex better than straight sex but couldn't handle being in a relationship with a man.

Nick watched Lucas as he looked around the room. He sighed and ran his fingers through the hair at the back of Lucas' head. Lucas turned to him. And smiled.

It looked good on Lucas. To see him so relaxed and happy.

"Meant to tell you," Lucas said and smirked. "I like your outfit."

Nick burst out laughing. Lucas was teasing him. His outfit was horrendous. He'd kept some of his old heavy metal clothes. Tight black leather pants. A black band t-shirt with holes in it. Low-slung metal studded black leather belt. Half a bucket of gel in his hair to keep it looking messed up, a vision of post-sex spikes. He had even kept his old black platform boots.

He wanted to rub his eyes. He wasn't used to wearing contacts. But his glasses didn't exactly fit the image he'd created with all the other gear. He'd even donned some black eyeliner.

"Your eyes look sexy," Lucas said.

"Noted." Nick smiled. "I'll hang onto the liner pencil." He leaned back and put his arm around Lucas' shoulders. Lucas placed his hand on Nick's thigh. This was nice. Sitting together out in public, not hiding their affection for one another. He could get used to this.

Lucas' phone dinged. He looked down at his screen scanning the text message. He nudged Nick, a big grin on his face. "Holy shit! Look at this!"

Lucas turned the screen to face Nick.

<Gary: Heard your single online.>

Lucas had sent a link to his song to every original content band he could think of that afternoon. They hadn't expected anyone would have listened to it already.

<Gary: Really liked it. We're looking for a sub for our rhythm guitarist. It would be a lot for you to learn but we'd be

thrilled to play your original stuff as well when you're playing.>

Nick looked up at Lucas. He gripped Lucas' face and kissed him. "That's amazing!"

"What should I say?"

"Are you up to learning some forty-odd songs?"

"It's doable."

"Then say *yes*. This is an awesome opportunity. I think you should go for it." Nick slipped his hands from Lucas' face. He'd overstepped by kissing Lucas like that. People were looking.

He'd been so excited for Lucas that he hadn't been able to stop himself.

A guy walked past their table.

"Faggots," he snarled.

Nick could see Lucas tense. He touched Lucas' arm. Lucas jerked away. His scowl was back. Hardcore. "Let it roll off you," Nick said.

"How?"

"People are going to say things to us. You need to accept that."

Lucas turned and glared at Nick. "I don't want to accept that." He rose to his feet.

Nick jumped up and stood beside him. "Please don't leave."

"I'm not leaving. I'm going to the washroom."

Nick looked around. The guy who had hurled the insult was nowhere in sight. He tugged on Lucas' sleeve. "Please don't engage with that guy if you see him."

"Not planning on it." A muscle in Lucas' jaw jumped as he scanned the bar. He was angry. Nick didn't want to leave him alone but it was time for him to go back on stage.

"Promise me."

Lucas stared at him, their eyes locked. Nick did his best to portray with his gaze that he was pleading with Lucas not to do anything stupid.

Lucas grunted. "Fine. I promise."

Two songs into the second set, Lucas came back to the table. He looked intact. If Lucas had run into the guy and he'd confronted him, it hadn't turned physical.

Lucas remained straight-faced for the remainder of the night's performance. During the second break, Lucas had monotone, monosyllabic answers in response to Nick's attempts at conversation.

Nick was glad to finish up the gig, get out of there, and into the fresh air.

Lucas still hadn't asked if he wanted to go back to his place.

They were halfway to Lucas' truck when a plodding group of heavy boots and grotesque anti-gay catcalls drifted toward them. They picked up their pace.

"Fuck," Nick whispered.

Nick looked over his shoulder. There were five guys. Big guys. He recognized them from the bar. "Do you remember *exactly* where your truck is?" he asked Lucas.

"Yeah," Lucas said as he snuck glances over his shoulder.

The calls became louder.

"Hey, little faggots!"

"Come and suck my dick!"

"We'll show you what a real man's cock feels like!"

This was bad. These weren't offhand, bigoted remarks. These guys were expressing an intention to do them some serious harm. He never should have kissed Lucas in that bar.

"Get ready to run," Nick whispered to Lucas.

He grabbed Lucas's arm. "Run!"

They took off running down the sidewalk at top speed. Switched to the road to avoid trees getting in their way. Nick dropped his guitar case. He didn't want the extra weight slowing him down. Lucas was lagging behind. Nick adjusted his speed so he wouldn't be separated from him. He could barely hear anything, his heart was beating so loud in his ears.

A swarm of thundering boots followed them.

Thwack. Thwack. Thwack. Thwack.

"Come back here you little shit eaters!"

"Gonna fuck you up!"

Nick's extremities started to go numb. Not a good time for his legs to give out. He grabbed Lucas' sleeve and hauled him along faster. They burst through the doors of the parking garage. Nick pushed the button on the elevator on the off chance it was on that floor.

No luck. They bolted up the stairs. Lucas's truck was on the 4th floor.

The pounding of ten heavy boots barreled up the stairs behind them. Nick took two stairs at a time. His vision was focused on each step ahead of him. He could hear Lucas right behind him. Lucas was panting and coughing. Nick's lungs were screaming.

He flung open the door to the 4th floor and they flew through the parking garage. Two clunks signaled Lucas had unlocked his truck. They both opened their doors so hard, they bashed the cars beside them. Doors slammed closed, Lucas locked them, and started the truck.

His tires screeched as Lucas backed the truck out of its spot. He nearly ran over the guys as he burned rubber toward the downramp. The thumping of their hands on the tailgate echoed throughout the cab of the truck. Lucas took each turn at top speed until they were on the street.

Lucas turned a corner, heading back in the direction of the bar. Nick's guitar case was in the middle of the street, scuffed from being booted down the street. Nick leaped out and collected it.

His favorite electric guitar was probably damaged.

Their lives were infinitely more important.

There was complete silence as they drove. Nick leaned against the truck door and looked out the window. They were headed for Oak Bay. Lucas was taking him home with him.

Lucas made no move to open his driver's side door after they pulled into his driveway.

"What are you thinking?" Nick asked.

Lucas turned and looked at Nick. "That I need you in my arms tonight."

"Okay. Let's do that." Nick opened his door. Lucas followed his lead and they made their way inside Lucas' house. By the time they got to the bedroom, they were both shaking, the adrenaline finally leaving their systems. They undressed. Nick fussed with his contacts, put them in a container he'd brought with him in his guitar case, and they climbed into bed.

Nick lay his head on Lucas' chest, his arm thrown over Lucas' abs. He nuzzled Lucas' skin with his cheek as Lucas tugged him into a desperate embrace.

Lucas kissed Nick's forehead.

"I was terrified something was going to happen to you," Lucas said.

"It was all my fault. I shouldn't have kissed you."

"You were excited for me. I'm not going to blame you for what happened."

"I should know better. I've been out for over twenty years."

"Complacency."

"Yeah. It feels so natural to touch someone I'm crazy about."

Lucas laughed against Nick's head. "Crazy, eh?"

Nick kissed Lucas' chest. "Okay, maybe only slightly insane."

Lucas' chest shook as a good laugh rolled through him. It made Nick grin. He lifted his head and let his gaze drift over Lucas' face in the dim illumination of a single lamp.

Lucas's personality was a perfect mix of dark and light.

Nick turned Lucas' face and kissed him. His mind blurred and his heart skipped a beat. He held Lucas' face and giggled against Lucas' lips. "Yeah, I think *crazy* was the right word."

"You're a nut bar." Lucas rolled Nick onto his back and hovered above him. "One I want to eat." He kissed the skin behind Nick's ear. "But where to start."

Lucas withdrew his hand from under Nick and turned Nick onto his stomach. He started at the base of Nick's neck. Tongue—lips—teeth. His left shoulder. Nipping and licking. Then the other shoulder. He licked Nick's spine between his shoulder blades.

Nick huffed a small laugh and jumped. Lucas' tongue tickled.

He squirmed as Lucas' tongue descended to his tailbone. Lucas bit one ass cheek and then the other. Nick gasped. His teeth felt so good. Then Lucas sucked where he had bitten him.

Nick jerked and groaned when Lucas' hand came down hard on his ass. Lucas took Nick's response as a positive sign. His hand came down on the other cheek. Lucas alternated sides until Nick's ass felt warm and each strike stung. Lucas leaned down and kissed his reddened skin.

"You needed that," Lucas said.

"I did." Nick had only been with one other guy willing to spank him. And he'd never paddled him hard enough. He suspected that wouldn't be a problem with Lucas.

Lucas spread Nick's legs and lay down between them. He

reached between Nick's ass cheeks, cupped his hard cock and balls, and shifted them down to lay out flat on the bedding, visible between his legs. Nick couldn't help but wonder where the hell Lucas had learned to do that.

That thought quickly left his mind.

Nick quivered and moaned when Lucas licked his shaft, the skin between his balls, and the crease of his ass. Lucas' strong hands separated his cheeks and his hot breath reached his hole.

Nick gripped his pillows and tucked his head against it, preparing himself.

The feel of Lucas' beard brushing his crease sent shivers through him. Lucas surged forward. The first lick was tentative and slow. Nick's throat emitted a low groan. He clutched tighter to the pillow. Lucas' face buried in his ass was going to take him to the very edge.

Lucas hooked a thumb in his hole and swept in with his tongue. With more urgency this time. He became like a man obsessed. Licking and sucking—and prodding.

Tongue and fingers.

Nick had never been eaten like this. Lucas' hunger was unprecedented. With his cock in that position, he wasn't able to grind into the bedding. That had been deliberate on Lucas' part.

Lucas abandoned his ass and licked his balls, then trailed his tongue down Nick's shaft. Lucas lifted his cock slightly with one hand and fed it into his mouth. He sucked slow and steady, clearing away any precum that had gathered at the tip. He rose on his knees and smacked Nick's ass.

"I want to top," Lucas said.

"I figured." Nick looked over his shoulder and grinned at Lucas, then lifted his hips and rearranged his cock so it was back under his belly.

Lucas climbed off the bed and dug around in a bedside dresser drawer.

He turned and scowled at Nick. "Plenty of lube. No condoms. Angie and I never used them."

"There's one in my wallet."

Nick licked his lips as he watched Lucas walk to the foot of the bed where Nick had abandoned his ridiculous leather pants. Lucas was gorgeous. Muscled—his thick cock piercing the air.

Lucas had a condom on by the time he returned to the bed. Nick stayed where he was. Sometimes he liked being fucked from behind. The thrusts hit all sorts of different spots.

Lucas shoved Nick's legs further apart and slathered a massive dollop of lube all over and in his hole. Then some on Lucas' cock. One of Lucas' hands came to rest to the left of Nick's hip.

Then he felt it. Lucas' cockhead breached his willing ring of slicked-up muscle. He bit the pillow. Lucas was big. He'd done a good job of prepping Nick, but nothing other than a sizeable butt plug could have prepared him for the burn in his ass and the pain racing up his spine.

Nick cried out and clung hard to the sheets, and Lucas slowed.

"Don't stop!" Nick stretched his arms out, took handfuls of sheets into his hands, and angled his hips to take Lucas all the way in. "Please. I need you to completely fill me."

Lucas straddled him with his arms, shoved Nick's legs further apart with his thighs, and advanced with a slow, steady pace until he was buried deep inside. Lucas' chest came to rest on Nick's back. He kissed Nick's shoulder and the back of his neck and withdrew his cock a short distance, then thrust back. Nick grunted. Another few thrusts and pain would turn to pleasure.

He just needed to breathe through it.

The weight of Lucas' body pressing him into the mattress was glorious. He felt protected from the world. It comforted him after the night they'd had—running for their lives.

Lucas growled in Nick's ear as he made another retreat and advance. Lucas reached out and covered Nick's hands. Hands that were stretched above his head with a death grip on the sheets. Lucas intertwined their fingers and he pumped his hips again. And again—and again.

There. Right there … the pleasure flowed in.

Lucas dug his knees into the mattress and changed the angle of his hips.

Oh, my god.

Faster and harder.

Lucas wasn't going to go easy on him. Every part of his body jolted forward, then settled back … then jolted forward again. Nick was having trouble catching his breath but he was riding on a high of exhilaration. Lucas was back on his hands so he could drill Nick harder.

Nick wanted more of him. Each pump of Lucas' hips set off a mad range of emotions and sensations. Lucas lowered himself onto his back again. This time, Lucas wrapped his arms around Nick's chest and settled his lips permanently against the skin between Nick's shoulders.

Lucas clung to Nick and cascaded.

"Nick! Fuck!"

Loud.

Uninhibited.

Unleashed.

Lucas squeezed Nick tighter as he pulsed into the condom. His kisses became more desperate. Nick loosened his grip on the sheets when Lucas started weeping.

Like full-on sobbing.

Nick struggled until he got free of Lucas' cock and out from under him.

"Jeezus, Lucas. What's wrong?"

Lucas rolled onto his back, fat tears streaming down his cheeks. He threw an arm over his eyes. "I've been having sex my entire adult life … and it has *never* felt like that."

Nick put his hand on Lucas' chest.

"Reality gave you another smack across the face?"

"Almost knocked me out," Lucas replied.

"You're gay."

"*So* gay." Lucas laughed softly. "Don't know why I got so emotional."

"Because this is pretty deep stuff. You're not who you thought you were."

"Not even close."

Nick was curious how far Lucas wanted to take that revelation.

"Have you thought about what you're going to tell your family?" Nick asked.

"Wow." Lucas brushed his hand across his eyes. "I have no idea."

"You know, you don't have to tell them. There are no rules when it comes to this."

Lucas turned and looked at Nick. "There may come a time when I want to introduce you to them. I want them to be prepared for that ahead of time."

"We're a long away from *meet the parents*."

"I know." Lucas ran his fingers down Nick's cheek and across his chin. "You're perfect. If the time comes, my family will love you."

Nick settled in against Lucas' chest and rode his moving arm for a few moments as Lucas fiddled with the condom and disposed of it off the side of the bed. Lucas was taking frightening leaps forward in his mind. They'd only been seeing each other for less than a week.

Lucas pulled the blankets over them and settled.

"You all right?" he asked.

"Other than the fact I won't be able to sit down for a week? Peachy." Nick snorted and giggled and tucked himself against Lucas' side.

"Your ass looked like a peach with beautiful shades of crimson on it."

"I liked it." He kissed Lucas' shoulder. "Maybe we can explore that some more?"

"Spanking?"

"Yeah."

"Sure. We can do that."

Nick's spirit soared. Someone he wasn't afraid to share his fantasies with lay beside him. A man who wanted to delve into a real relationship with him. It was more than a dream.

Lucas pulled away from Nick and drifted down his body. This time, Nick didn't deprive Lucas of his cock when he came. Lucas sucked him hard through his entire climax.

With an exhausted groan, Lucas crawled back up the bed to hold him.

Nick tried to stay awake. To enjoy Lucas' scent. The sound of him breathing. The way Lucas' arms wrapped around him. The final sweet, loving kiss before they fell asleep.

Chapter Seven | Lucas

Waking up with Nick in his arms was surreal. This was the same bed that had seen years of intimacy distance and disappointment. None of that had happened last night.

Lucas lay still, listening to the sound of Nick's sleeping breaths. This man had changed his entire world. Nick had stirred up an incredible desire in him and a longing to be closer to him.

After countless failed relationships, Lucas actually saw this one going somewhere. They had so much in common with their music. And the sex was amazing. Gut-wrenching amazing.

Last night's frightening experience had thrown him off, though. What happened had been some of his worst fears realized, that he was putting himself in danger by being gay.

His heart thudded in his chest as he looked at Nick. They were possibly headed for a loving relationship. If not Nick, then some other guy might eventually come along.

Did he want to do that? To put himself in harm's way.

If he didn't, he might spend his life never knowing true love. Was he willing to sacrifice that possibility of love to avoid incidents like last night?

He clapped a hand over his eyes.

Last night—he'd been terrified. That hoard of men had been threatening to beat them … and possibly rape them. They were two against five. They wouldn't have been able to fight them off.

Lucas slipped out from underneath Nick and headed into the kitchen for a glass of water. He leaned against the counter and stared at the ceiling with tears in his eyes.

He wasn't sure he could do this with Nick.

Buried deep in the closet, he was cozy and safe. No one was threatening him in there. But it was also lonely in there.

Fuck.

He wasn't sure what to do.

"Hey." Nick wandered into the kitchen only wearing underwear. He looked adorable. His hair was a complete mess of gel and bedhead. His eyes were rimmed in smeared black eyeliner.

"It's early. Why are you up?" Nick asked.

"Water." Lucas wiped the dampness from his eyes and raised his glass. "Want one?"

Nick bit his bottom lip as he looked at Lucas. Lucas hadn't bothered with any clothes at all. "Yeah, water … that's what I want." He winked at Lucas.

"Getting you one anyway." Lucas retrieved the filtered water container from the fridge and poured Nick a glass. Nick drained the glass in one go.

"We need to talk about last night," Lucas said. He had a decision floating on the edge of his consciousness. They were less than a week into this relationship. It was still early enough.

Nick set his glass on the counter. "I've never had that happen before. Sure guys have threatened me but never like that. That's not normal … please don't think it is."

Lucas crossed his arms when Nick moved to approach him.

"Wow, okay. What?" Nick said.

"I'm having reservations."

"About what? About us or being gay?"

"Both."

Nick gripped Lucas's crossed arms. "But last night, you sounded like you were all in."

Lucas hated the look on Nick's face. He'd devastated the gentle, exuberant man who had been at his side as he discovered himself—the man who had brought some joy into his life.

Nick tipped his head to one side. Tears gathered at the corners of his eyes. "Please don't do this to me—to us." He squeezed Lucas' arms. "We're so good together."

Lucas softened and pulled Nick into his arms. How could he possibly let this man go? They were *more* than good together—they were perfect together. He might have a future with him. A future full of love and Nick's laughter. For the first time in his life, he might find himself happy.

"No more kissing in public. Or holding hands or anything," Lucas said. He could feel Nick's body stiffen. But it had to be this way. They couldn't risk their lives again.

Nick sniffed. "Not sure I can do that." He looked up at Lucas. "And how long would this restriction last? A month? A year? Until after we're married? When we have kids?"

The most Lucas could do was blink. That was a lot of speculation. Married? Kids? Neither of those things were on his radar. He wasn't sure how to answer Nick.

"I'm sorry," Nick said. "I didn't mean to dump that on you."

"No, I get it. I wouldn't want it to be forever."

"Then why do it now?"

Lucas dipped his head and kissed Nick's head. "I couldn't bear it if you were hurt."

"We just have to be more careful. More selective about where we are."

"I don't know, Nick. We're taking chances."

Nick snuggled into Lucas' embrace. He felt so good in

Lucas's arms. Nick traced a finger down Lucas' chest. "Okay, no kissing. But I still want to be able to hold your hand."

Lucas sighed. It was a compromise he could live with. As long as they made sure they were in a safe space before showing any affection. Before allowing people to see they were together.

Nick stepped away and hauled on Lucas' arm. "Come on. I'm tired. Come back to bed."

Lucas smirked and followed Nick back to the bedroom. It felt good, arranging himself under the covers with Nick tucked against him. He clung to him and inhaled the scent of him.

He could easily fall asleep to that scent for the rest of his life.

They finished playing his song and you could feel the exhilaration in the air. It had been played to perfection. That one song of Lucas' had never sounded so good. He turned to each band member. They were all smiling and laughing. It was sweet when everything came together like that. Not a single mistake; musical instruments and vocals in perfect harmony.

This was the third practice Lucas had been invited to with the band that was willing to play his original music on the nights he was on stage. They had learned five of his songs. He had learned all thirty-two of theirs. It had been a month since they first contacted him.

The same night he and Nick had been chased by a mob of bigoted thugs.

He'd been seeing Nick for just over a month now. They'd grown incredibly close. Spent more days together than apart most weeks. They'd given up on calling any nights they went out together dates. They were just them and they hung around most nights if they weren't gigging.

"I think we have that one," Gary the leader of the band said. "Sound good to you, Lucas?"

"Sounds just like I imagined it."

"Perfect."

A familiar voice over his shoulder. "Sounded good out here."

Lucas pivoted and smiled at Nick. He'd asked Nick to meet him after the practice. He must have come in and he hadn't noticed him arrive while they were playing.

"Hey," Gary said. "Nick, right? You're the guy who's been taking the busking scene by storm."

Nick laughed. "That would be me." He pointed at Lucas. "I've been helping Lucas record some of his songs. Very cool to hear one live."

"You're welcome to stick around," Gary said.

"Thanks. Lucas and I are heading out tonight so that works for me." Nick took a seat on an old sofa in the corner of the room. The practice space was the back room of a woodworking shop. The drum kit and every other surface was always covered in dust, but it was cheap to rent.

Gary nodded and suggested the next song they needed to work on. Lucas had been playing it for Nick this afternoon during one of their regular duo jam sessions.

Nick had leaned across Lucas' guitar and kissed him after he finished playing it. Lucas smiled as he played his sections. It had been one of Nick's bone-melting kisses.

They'd ended up back in bed after that.

With Nick, all of Lucas' old conceptions of being impotent had been burned to the ground. They could be all over each other multiple times a day and not get tired.

They finished the practice. Nick had only been made to wait for an hour. Lucas knew that wasn't a hardship for him.

Nick was never bored by music.

"So, Lucas," Gary said. "This Friday. You ready?"

"8 pm. I'll be there." Lucas turned to Nick. "Babe, you working Friday?"

A chill ran up Lucas' spine. He hadn't meant to say use that word *babe*. It had slipped out. They'd both fallen into using the term of affection over the past couple of weeks.

He hadn't told Gary and the band he was gay. Why would he? It was his personal business. He hadn't even officially told the bass player of his own band, but Samuel had worked it out the first time he and Nick held hands at the band table. Their joined hands had received a brief look from Samuel and a shrug. It had given Lucas a lot of confidence in his relationship with Nick.

Gary scowled at Lucas. He pointed at Nick. "You two together?"

No point in denying it now. "For just over a month," Lucas answered.

Gary crossed his arms. "I don't want any trouble. Some of us heard what happened to Nick. Didn't realize you were the other guy, Lucas. I don't want any disruptions in our show."

"There won't be." A quiver ran up the back of Lucas' legs. He couldn't lose this opportunity to get his music out there in front of an audience. He looked at Nick. They were becoming serious but music would always come first in his life. "Nick and I won't let on we're together."

"I'm holding you to that," Gary said. "One single issue and you're out."

Fuck.

Lucas packed away his guitar and fumbled with the latches. He was shaking. He couldn't fuck this up. Gary had even talked about touring with him playing in the band during the summer.

The possibility of playing his own music to a wider audience was a dream come true.

He could tell Nick wasn't impressed by what he had promised Gary. But he didn't have a choice. Music was his life. Nick led the way out to Lucas' truck.

"You take a taxi to get here?" Lucas asked.

"Yeah." Nick climbed up into the passenger seat, whipped his seatbelt out, and clicked it in place. He crossed his arms. He was annoyed. "So, we're going to be doing it your way after all."

"What do you mean?"

"No kissing. No touching. No lingering looks."

"I can't lose this gig, Nick."

Nick stared at him. "But you're willing to lose me."

"Ah, come on." This was ridiculous. Lucas started the truck. "You're telling me you're going to walk because I won't hold your hand in public? What are you, five?"

"I'm thirty-five and I'm too old to put up with this kind of shit?"

"Oh, my career is *this kind of shit* now, is it?

"I thought we'd grown closer than that."

"We have grown closer." Lucas turned and put his hand on Nick's thigh. "You have no idea how much you mean to me."

"That's because you never tell me."

"Look who's talking."

Nick's brow dipped and he glared at Lucas. "Okay. How's this for telling you. I'm falling in love with you, all right? Is that satisfactory enough when it comes to telling you how I feel?"

Lucas slammed his palms against the steering wheel.

Jeezus Christ.

How did he end up here? He was not going to be coerced

into choosing between Nick and music. Even if Nick *was* falling in love with him, Nick wouldn't win this battle.

"Music comes first, Nick. You know that."

"Over me."

"Yes, even over you."

Nick whipped off his seatbelt, flung his door open, and leaped out. "Fuck you!" He stormed off across the parking lot, swearing and shouting. Lucas thought about going after him.

But why? Lucas had made up his mind. Music came first.

He had to stretch to close the passenger door, then tore out of the lot, and headed toward home. He still had some songs to perfect and only a few nights to do it. He was not expecting the absolute wallop of despair to hit him as he walked in through his front door.

Just this morning, he and Nick had been laughing and collaborating on a few tunes. Things had gotten silly and they'd ended up making out on the sofa.

He stared at that sofa.

No. He was holding firm on this. He wasn't throwing this chance away over a guy. Even if that guy was Nick. He slumped onto the sofa and ran his hands through his hair.

Fuck, his life was going to feel empty without him.

Maybe he had been falling in love too. What he was feeling was more than simple attraction. He and Nick had grown their relationship into something special.

He groaned.

Oh, my god. I have.

I'm not just falling.

I've fallen.

"Fuck!"

Lucas stormed into the kitchen, threw open the fridge, and grabbed a beer. Maybe if he drank enough, and shouted at the ceiling for the rest of the night, he could get Nick out of his system.

The first idea and the second didn't work. He just woke up the next morning with a throbbing headache and a sore throat. And the distinct sensation he had made a horrible mistake.

Chapter Eight | Nick

Nick pulled up outside his sister's house. She'd said to come on over when he'd phoned her messy crying. He'd called to talk things through with her and had ended up breaking down.

There was no requirement to knock on her door. His sister Nicole had an open-door policy when it came to family. He walked in, called her name, and followed her response into the kitchen. She was in the midst of making cookies. Her five kids were constantly hungry.

Nick had held out as long as possible before phoning Nicole. It had been over three weeks since he'd told Lucas to *fuck off*. He'd honestly believed Lucas would cave and phone him.

Word in the music community was that Lucas' original songs were being well received. Next month, in June, the band Lucas was subbing for was going on tour. He was going with them.

They'd be gone for 6 weeks.

"What's up with this guy, little brother? Why the sobbing?"

Nick slid onto a stool at the marble-countered island. Nicole and her husband did well money-wise. Her husband was a surgeon and Nicole was a biology professor at UVIC. University was off for the summer. It was a perfect schedule for her to spend more time with their kids.

Their house was gorgeous.

"I was falling in love with him. That's what's up."

"What's his name?"

"Lucas."

"Where did you meet him?"

"Deckers. I was working sound. He's in a band."

Nicole pulled a tray of cookies from the oven and replaced it with a second tray. They looked to be chocolate chip. She scrapped one off the baking tray and deposited it in front of Nick.

"Have a warm cookie."

Not going to help. But it tasted amazing. He slipped off the stool and fetched himself a glass of milk. Yeah, sometimes, he was a child. He dipped a second cookie into the milk.

"Did that work for you? Him being in a band?" Nicole asked.

"We spent a lot of time down in my studio jamming and recording music. We went to each other's shows when we could and hung out with other bands most nights."

"Good match, then?"

"Perfect match." Nick brushed some of the cookie crumbs off his hands. "And the sex … oh my god, Nicole. I've never felt so connected with someone in my life."

"He bisexual too?"

Nick shook his head. "No, he's gay."

"So what happened between you?"

"Like I said on the phone. He told me music was more important than me."

"And you don't feel the same way about your music?"

Nick sighed. "I thought I did until I started dating him."

"You'd give up music for him?"

"I wouldn't go that far. But I'd certainly make him my priority."

"You sure you don't love him already?"

"Fuck … I don't know, Nicole." Nick propped his head in

his hand. "Oh, my god. I do."

"What are you going to do about it?"

"What can I do? He's made his position quite clear. Music is more important than me. And the fact he was able to say that to me with a straight face makes me not want to reconcile even if he wanted to. These past few weeks have given me time to think. I need someone who is going to prioritize me over anything else .. even music. I deserve that."

"You wouldn't go back to him?"

"Why? So he can break my heart again the next time he swings back to music as his love."

"So … move on. There must be other guys or women out there."

"I don't know." Nick rubbed his forehead. "There's a guy who's been chatting me up."

"Call him. Get out of this depressing rut you're wallowing in."

Three weeks. Was that too soon to move on? Lucas wasn't going to phone or text him, that's for sure. It really was over. The guy who had been hitting on him and dropping all sorts of obvious hints was in a committed relationship with a husband and they were looking for a third.

A night of ménage might be exactly what he needed to get Lucas off his mind. He sent the guy a text asking when they wanted to meet. He answered. They wanted to grab a drink at a bar out in Langford before they all headed back to their place. To make sure they were compatible.

Nick blew out a gust of air and set his phone on the counter facedown.

"Okay, done," Nick said to Nicole. "I'm meeting him tonight." He sure as hell wasn't going to tell his sister he'd made a date with two guys. There were some things she didn't need to know. It would be a first for him but he was looking forward to a complete distraction.

"Good."

Nick rose and shoved the stool back under the countertop. "I'll get out of your hair and go get ready for my date." In other words a thorough douching. His ass was going to get seriously used tonight. His cock pulsed and swelled. He was so ready to get back into bed with someone.

Nick met the guys outside a bar he'd never been to before. He still hadn't ventured far beyond downtown in his travels. He wasn't planning on moving away. He had plenty of time to get to know the suburbs better. He especially wanted to head out to the Sooke potholes.

Both guys were gorgeous. Late 40s. Keith and Daryl. They'd been together for over twenty years. Their relationship had always been open and they often brought in a third. It worked for them. As they approached the front doors, Nick noticed the sandwich board outside.

Friday night
Mystic Blues
Playing 9 pm – 12:30 am

"Um," Nick turned to Keith. "Can we go somewhere else?"

"No," Daryl said. "We came here because of this band. We've seen them a bunch of times and like their vibe. You have a problem with that?"

Nick swallowed. "No." *Mystic Blues*. That was the band that had brought Lucas on to cover when their rhythm guitarist couldn't make it. It was unlikely Lucas was playing.

He followed the guys into the bar. They headed straight for the stage area. They had reserved a table right up front so they could see the band. Nick scanned the stage and exhaled a sigh.

There was no Lucas.

Keith and Daryl moved the chairs around so all three of them were facing forward and sandwiched Nick in between them. The conversation was light as they waited for the band to start.

During the sound check, Keith leaned toward Nick, close to his ear.

"So, what kind of things are you into?"

Nick licked his lips. This could get interesting. "I'm vers."

Keith smiled as he leaned back. "Perfect. I'm a top. Daryl is a bottom. You can play with both of us separately. We both like to watch the other one fucking."

"Toys?" Keith asked. "Plugs? A fat, long dragon dildo?"

Dragon? That was new for him. Sounded fun.

"Sure," he answered.

"Double penetration,? Daryl asked.

Well, shit.

"With enough prep, I'm game," Nick answered.

"Paddles, ball gags, and handcuffs?'

"I love a good submissive spanking," Nick replied.

"Cum play?"

Nick smiled. "Love it."

"Do you mind staying with us all night?'

"I've got nowhere else be," Nick replied.

Keith grinned. "Fuck. I am going to fuck every conscious thought out of your head."

Nick laughed. "Perfect."

With all this sex talk, Nick's cock was throbbing. He didn't even notice that the band had started playing. He was ready to get out of there and head to their place.

Keith lifted his hand, placed it at the base of Nick's neck, and played with his hair. Nick leaned into Keith's palm and almost moaned aloud. It had been too long since he'd had any human contact.

Daryl's hand came to rest on Nick's thigh. It cruised up until his warm fingers were fondling Nick's hard cock through his jeans. "You're so hard," Daryl said close to his ear.

"All that talk turned me on," Nick answered. He knew his face was going to be showing his growing desire. As the men caressed him, he could barely keep his eyes open.

He was fucking floating in a cloud of lust in public.

Nick looked up at the band. His gaze wandered to the far left where the rhythm guitarist would be. His heart froze—stopped fucking beating.

Lucas was standing there, staring at him with such sadness in his eyes that Nick thought his heart would never start again. He pushed Daryl's hand off him and shrugged away from Keith.

"What's the matter?" Keith asked.

"It's my ex-boyfriend." Nick jerked his head in Lucas' direction. "My ex-boyfriend is playing up there. I don't want him to see you two manhandling me."

Nick's gaze met Lucas' and tears formed in Nick's eyes.

He *was* in love with the guy. Nick started shaking, then burst up from his seat, pushing Daryl out of the way so he could get out. He ran to the washroom and broke down in front of the sinks.

He'd never cried as much in his life as he had in the past three weeks. He splashed some cold water on his face to try and calm himself.

He was not expecting to hear the soft, sexy voice approaching.

"Nick."

Nick whipped around. "You're supposed to be on stage."

"Fuck that. What the hell were you doing with those two guys?"

"I'm on a date."

There was that sadness again written all over Lucas' expression. He scowled and stared at the floor. "Is that what you're doing now? Fucking more than one guy at a time?"

Nick put his hands on his hips. "So what if I am?" Lucas had no right to snoop around in his personal life. He gave up that privilege when he chose music over him.

Then what the hell was he doing in the washroom while his band was playing?

"Seriously," Nick said. "Shouldn't you be up with the band?"

"I saw you with those two … what they were doing to you."

"And?" Nick crossed his arms. "We're not together anymore, remember? You decided your music career was more important than me. More important than us."

"I still care about you."

"Care? That's where you got to after all the time we spent together. You *care* about me?"

"Where was I supposed to get to?"

"Fuck you." Nick turned back toward the sink. He could see Lucas in the mirror walking closer to him. He shivered when Lucas put his hand on his shoulder.

God, I miss him touching me.

"Are you *with* them?" Lucas asked.

"None of your fucking business."

"Nick, don't do it if it's random," Lucas said. "I don't want that for you."

"You don't get to decide what I do. If I want to fuck two guys, that's what I'm going to do."

Lucas stepped closer and kissed the back of Nick's neck.

"Please don't do it." Nick gripped the countertop. Lucas' lips on him made it difficult to stay upright.

And Lucas was lingering. His breath was hot on Nick's neck.

"You have no say," Nick whispered.

Lucas moved his hand from Nick's shoulder. Nick sucked in a gasp as Lucas wrapped his arms around Nick's waist. Lucas nuzzled the side of Nick's neck.

"What are you doing?" Nick asked but didn't pull away. How could he? He'd dreamed of having Lucas' arms around him again. He couldn't walk away from his embrace.

"I miss you so much," Lucas whispered.

"You didn't want me."

"That's not true."

"You chose playing your originals over me, Lucas." Nick turned in Lucas' arms so he was facing him. Their noses were nearly touching. Lucas didn't loosen his grasp on him. Lucas had developed serious feelings for him. It was obvious by the way he was holding him.

There was love there.

Lucas studied Nick's eyes. "I made a mistake."

Nick put his hands on Lucas' chest and shoved him away. "You don't get to do that. You don't get to push me away, not call me, not text me, and then when I show up with someone other than you, you decide you made a mistake. I don't believe you."

"What do I have to do to make you believe me?"

Nick crossed his arms. "Tell me how you really felt about me when we were together."

Lucas scowled and used his eyes to plead with Nick. He couldn't say it. Lucas wandered back toward Nick. "You know. You know how I felt about you. How I feel about you."

Love.

"I need you to say it."

Lucas' chest was heaving. He licked his lips, stepped close to Nick, and took Nick's face in his hands. Nick almost pushed him away but the look in Lucas' eyes kept him from doing it.

"Say it," Nick reiterated.

Lucas swallowed. "Nick … Fuck." He looked at the floor, then back at Nick. "Can I kiss you first? I need to know you're open to what I want to say to you."

Nick scowled at Lucas. "What the fuck, Lucas. You can't say it, can you?" He pushed Lucas away from him. "I don't have time for you. I have two hot men waiting for me."

He headed for the door and flung it open. He wasn't sure if Lucas followed him or not. He beelined it back to his table. Keith and Daryl looked concerned as he sat back in his chair.

"Can we go?" Nick asked and put a hand on each of their thighs.

"I'm horny," he lied.

They were about to get up and leave when Lucas dashed in front of the table. He looked like a wild man. He'd obviously been jamming his hands into his hair. His eyes looked desperate.

He gripped the table.

"Don't go with them, Nick," Lucas said. "Please."

"Why not?"

"Fuck, Nick. You know why."

"Say it," Nick demanded. If Lucas couldn't say it, they were done for good.

Lucas sank to his knees on the floor in front of the table. His arms slipped from the table to his thighs. Tears formed in his eyes until one escaped down his cheek.

He stared at Nick and blinked once.

His lips moved to form words, then he hesitated and looked at the floor.

Jeezus Christ.

"We're done, Lucas." Nick shoved his way past Daryl and headed for the door. He could hear Lucas sobbing and swearing above the sound of the music. Everyone in the bar could hear him.

Nick put his hand on the handle of the door. Once he walked out that door, it was over. Keith and Daryl joined him. They each put a hand on the center of his back to usher him out.

"Nick!" Lucas hollered from his place on the floor in front of the stage. "Please don't!"

Nick exhaled a long breath and turned away from the door to face Lucas.

"Why?" he shouted.

A sob from Lucas. "Because I fucking love you, Nick!"

Nick nearly crumpled but he couldn't run fast enough to join Lucas on the floor. He threw his arms around Lucas, gripped his face, and kissed him. All the pieces of his broken heart found their way back home. He was filled with feelings of devotion. He was never going to leave this man.

Lucas could shut down and push all he wanted. Now that he knew Lucas loved him, he would never let Lucas succeed in challenging what they shared ever again.

He pulled his lips away from Lucas' but still held his face. "I love you too."

The music stopped playing.

"We're going to take a little break here, folks," Gary said. "Back in twenty minutes." He jumped off the stage and approached them. He looked down at Lucas. "I think it goes without saying … you're fired. Grab your shit off the stage."

Then Gary shook his head and walked away.

Lucas rose to his feet and went to the stage. He unplugged and grabbed his guitar and hauled his amplifier to his thigh. He handed Nick his guitar and Nick put it in its case.

Everything collected, Nick put his hand on Lucas' shoulder. "You all right?"

"I'll survive." Lucas walked toward the door. Keith and Daryl had reseated themselves at the table. Nick only glanced in their direction on their way out. He probably wouldn't have been able to go through with it. Lucas would have been on his mind. It would have felt like he was cheating.

Nick loaded Lucas' guitar into Lucas' truck. "I have my car here. Where are we going?"

"Can we go out for coffee?"

"Lorraine's Café? It's the only one I can think of that's open at night."

Lucas nodded. "Sure. Meet you there."

It felt strange driving away in a different car than Lucas. As if he had imagined the whole incident at the bar. The very public declaration of love. There was a sliver of doubt in his gut that wondered if he'd arrive at the café and Lucas wouldn't show up.

He relaxed as Lucas pulled into the parking lot behind him.

They entered the café together and found a quiet booth away from other people. Coffee and pie were ordered and delivered, and they were finally left alone.

"Where do we go from?" Nick asked.

Lucas set his gaze on Nick's eyes. "I'm not sure. I think I just blew up my musical career."

"You have your cover band still. As for originals, I'm sure another band will pick you up. I don't think you have to worry about that."

Lucas nodded. "You're probably right."

"But you certainly blew up what you had for me." Nick reached for Lucas' hand. They held hands across the table from one another. "You surprised me. I didn't think you'd do it."

Lucas furrowed his brow. "When I saw you with those two guys, it hit me how much I loved and missed you and what an idiot I'd been for letting you go like that."

"We were both idiots, but you running back to the closet and restricting any public affection primed me for ending things with you. Not going to lie, I was ready to bolt, regardless of my feelings for you. Then you pushed hard telling me I wasn't as important as your music."

"I was wrong."

"And I was wrong running from you. I should have fought for us."

"We both fucked up," Lucas said.

"So … where *do* we go from here?"

"Can we start dating again?"

Nick nodded. He agreed with Lucas. They needed to take it slow until they trusted each other again. "I think that's a good place to start. And keep sex off the table for now."

Lucas tucked his bottom lip against his teeth. "Yeah. Okay."

They'd have to reconcile strictly on spending time with each other. Talking. Hanging out. Finding out more about each other. The physical connection would have to wait until later.

Chapter Nine | Lucas

It had been over a month since he and Nick had agreed to date again. They had started with once a week. Once a week had led to twice. Twice had led to three times a week. They'd had some incredible makeout sessions but they'd stuck to their restriction on sex.

They'd never been closer. Lucas had found out so much about Nick and his life. He was incredibly close to his sister. Not so much with his parents. They were disappointed that Nick hadn't pursued his original career plan of becoming a registered nurse. They hoped his music was a passing phase and he would eventually come to his senses.

They covered all sorts of likes and dislikes. Childhood antics. Holiday adventures. The trouble they had gotten into as teens that made them wonder how they were still alive. Friends they'd had along the way. Favorite foods. Philosophical beliefs. General wants and needs. Kinks.

Lucas had finally felt comfortable opening up to Nick about his young life. His dad had been away on business trips for most of his upbringing. His mom had essentially been a single mom. He and his brother had been a handful on top of their mom's full-time job and Lucas and his brother had spent a lot of their time alone and fending for themselves.

The lack of parental guidance had made Lucas angry and resentful. And when their parents were home, they never showed any kind of affection. Lucas had never been told he was loved.

Nick saying he loved him every time they were together still felt surreal. He'd honestly thought he wasn't lovable. He and Angie had sometimes exchanged words of love.

But neither one of them had meant it.

Being loved felt more than good. Being able to tell someone he loved them even better. He'd been so terrified to say it. To open himself up to being rejected for expressing it. When Nick had demanded he say it—all he'd felt was panic. The love had been hidden behind a steel door.

It wasn't until Nick was walking out of the bar with those two guys that he'd felt entirely compelled to rip that steel door open. The thought of someone other than him tasting Nick's skin, when he loved every square inch of it—the panic had handed him a crowbar.

Sobbing and breaking down, he'd used it.

He'd never told anyone he loved them before and meant it. The resistance as he'd worked on that steel barrier had shredded his insides, he'd been so frantic to say it.

To tell Nick he loved him.

Now, he said it every single day. And the feeling came from deep within his heart.

Undeniable.

Lucas held Nick's hand as they pulled up in front of Nick's sister's house. This was a huge step for both of them. He felt as though he knew Nick's sister Nicole well already but he'd never met her. Nick's parents would be there as well. And aunts, uncles, and cousins.

It was a big family gathering, an annual barbeque in his sister's extensive backyard. It was a cool summer but warm enough that it was pleasant to be outside.

Nick gripped Lucas' hand as they entered the backyard through a high gate. The first people Nick spotted were his parents. Lucas clung tight to Nick's hand. This was so incredibly important, that they liked him. He was in love with their son. He needed to be good enough in their eyes.

"Mom. Dad." Nick released Lucas' hand, ran up, hugged his mom, and shook his dad's hand. Then Nick was right back with Lucas, holding his hand again. He lifted their joined hands, kissed Lucas's knuckles, and smiled at him. It made Lucas feel better. Nick was proud to be with him.

"This is Lucas." Nick grinned at his parents. "The incredible guy I'm in love with."

Nick's dad stepped forward and offered his hand to Lucas. "We've heard a lot about you." He laughed. "Soooo much. You can call me Earl." Lucas shook Earl's hand.

"Our Nicky can't stop talking about you," Nick's mom said. "I'm Natalie."

"It's nice to meet you both."

"All right," A very beautiful, very pregnant woman approached them. Lucas would have mistaken her and Nick for twins if he hadn't known she was his big sister. "Is this the guy you won't shut up about?" Nicole brought Lucas in for a hug. "He's been driving us crazy."

"What can I say," Nick said. "I'm smitten."

Nicole laughed. "More like ga-ga in love." She linked arms with Lucas and gave him a little tug. "Come inside and help me get the meat organized for the grill."

Lucas gave Nick a frightened look as Nicole hauled him across the yard and into the house. It was a gorgeous kitchen she pulled him into. She handed him a plastic container from the fridge.

"Lift the steaks out of there and put them on this plate." She set a plate in front of him. "And tell me more about you and Nick. You really hurt him a while back."

"I know." Lucas cleared his throat. "I was an idiot. He's the best thing that has ever happened to me. And for some ridiculous reason, I was prepared to throw away what we had together over a handful of songs. Songs I have since started performing with another band."

"Yeah, Nick told me you found a band that doesn't care that you two are together."

Lucas used the fork Nicole had provided to place each steak on the plate. They looked well-marinated and delicious. He hoped she wasn't planning on overcooking them.

"I can grill these if you want," Lucas said.

"My husband usually does it, but I'm sure he won't mind. He's busy talking to our uncle about some business deal he's working on."

"What kind of business? I thought he was a surgeon."

"Medical supplies."

Lucas must have made a face because Nicole laughed. "Yeah, I know. Really exciting."

"To each their own."

"Nick says you work in construction?"

Lucas took the plate and followed Nicole back into the yard and toward the grilling area which was essentially an outdoor kitchen.

"Not a chosen career. Fell into it because my brother works for them."

"You don't like it?"

"I'd rather do music full time."

"Like Nick."

"Yeah, he's got a pretty sweet deal mixing sound jobs with his busking."

"Did he tell you about his gay erotica audio work?"

Lucas' eyebrows rose. "No, he did not."

Nicole burst out laughing. "You'll have to listen to some of the audiobooks. He read some gay erotica short stories for a local author. They're an absolute riot."

Lucas smirked. "*That* is going to be our next date night." The grill reached the perfect temperature so Lucas put the steaks on to sear on one side, then flipped them over.

"Medium rare," Nicole said. "Unless you want yours more raw or tough as an old boot."

"No, medium rare is perfect."

"Then I'll leave it to you." Nicole smiled, patted his arm, and started shouting at one of the kids to get out of the vegetable garden.

"Can I get you a beer?" Nick sidled up next to Lucas and kissed him on the cheek.

"I'd love one."

"Be right back."

As he was cooking, Lucas looked out over the yard. At least nine children were ripping around the lawn, chasing a ball, the youngest a toddler barely keeping up. Nick's parents were talking and laughing with another couple Lucas assumed were Nick's mom's sister and her wife. And there were a few others Nick's age, maybe Nick's cousins whom he'd likely meet soon.

He liked that Nick's aunt was a lesbian in a committed relationship. It made him feel more comfortable knowing they were accepted in Nick's family.

"Here you go." Nick handed Lucas an open beer. "Nicole must trust you. Those steaks are sacred in the family barbeque. Please don't overcook them."

"I won't. I'm good on the grill."

Nick hugged Lucas around the waist. "You're good at a lot of things."

Lucas snorted. "What's that supposed to mean?" He flipped

the steaks over. 2 more minutes a side and they'd be done. He retrieved a clean plate from a shelf to the left of the grill.

Nicole was busy putting salads, buns, and cutlery on the large table Lucas assumed they had hauled out from the dining room. There was enough seating for everyone except the older kids. There were colorful, square fold-up tables scattered about the yard for them.

"It means," Nick answered, "I think we should revisit a restriction we've had."

Lucas nearly dropped the plate of steaks.

"Sex," he whispered.

"I was thinking … after the barbeque, we could go and get reacquainted with each other back at your place. Spend the night. Do a little tasting and exploring."

Lucas couldn't believe he was hesitating but he wanted Nick to be sure. They'd had a whole month of trust-building that had brought them closer together. He loved Nick more than ever.

Then why the hesitation?

He needed to trust Nick with this too.

"You're sure," Lucas said and cupped Nick's face. They moved apart for a second when Nicole offered her apologies for interrupting and grabbed some napkins.

"I've missed the feel of you against my skin," Nick said. "I need you to rock me into the mattress and wake up with me tomorrow. I need to spend the morning making love to you."

Lucas licked his lips. "How long do we have to stay here?"

Nick laughed. "Another couple of hours at least."

Lucas groaned which sent Nick into a fit of giggles. Hand in hand they found their seats at the table and dug into the food. Halfway through dinner, Nick decided he didn't want the mushrooms on his plate. Lucas was happy to eat them for him.

He wasn't sure why Nick had taken them.

Nick hated asparagus, cilantro, celery, and mushrooms.

As Lucas picked the mushrooms off Nick's plate and ate them, Lucas caught Nicole looking at him, smiling. She winked at him and raised her glass of water with a nod in his direction.

Stamp of approval.

That's what that was.

Lucas grinned at Nick's animated profile and kissed his shoulder. Nick was busy talking to his lesbian aunt but he reached over and placed his hand on Lucas' thigh. Nick had explained that even though she was younger than a lot of the women in his family, his sister Nicole was the matriarch. Her opinion of him would set the tone for the rest of the family.

And she'd deemed him worthy.

Dessert was loaded onto the table and he and Nick insisted on trying everything—twice. As he was finishing his last serving of tiramisu, his phone rang.

He excused himself from the table before he answered the call. The call display said VIHA. The Vancouver Island Health Authority. His palms started to sweat. "Hello?"

"Hi, this is Royal Jubilee ER. Is this Lucas?"

"Yes."

"Your brother, Eric, has been brought in to us. You're his emergency contact on file."

Fuck.

Lucas paced further away from the table.

"What happened?"

"Your brother was involved in an accident at work this afternoon."

And they're just calling me now?

"How bad?"

"He's stable but he'll be going into surgery soon."

"Please tell me ... how bad is he?"

There was a long pause on the other end of the line. "His injuries are life-threatening. But we'll be able to tell you more once we get in there and assess the damage."

Nick tugged on Lucas' sleeve. "What's wrong?"

Lucas covered the microphone. "Eric. He was hurt at work. It's bad."

"Then we should go." Nick clung to Lucas' shirt.

"We'll be right there," Lucas said into his phone.

Nick made their apologies for leaving. Told everyone it was an emergency and he'd let them know what was happening when he knew something. It didn't feel strange, having all of those people worried about his brother. Nick was his family and Nick's family was now his family.

Lucas let Nick drive his truck to the hospital. His nerves were too much of a mess to concentrate on driving. It seemed to take forever to park and walk to the emergency room.

The greeting *ambassador* picked up a clipboard and met them at the start of the line.

"What brings you in today?"

"My brother ...," Lucas started then struggled through a sob.

"My boyfriend's brother was brought in. Eric Peterson. He's going into surgery."

"They'll have moved him out of the ER by now." The ambassador pointed at a bank of plastic seating. "If you take a seat, I'll find out where a good place would be for you to wait."

They found two seats together and once they dropped onto the uncomfortable bucket chairs, Nick grabbed Lucas' hand and squeezed it. "Everything is going to be all right."

"We don't know that."

"No, but we can put it out into the universe."

Lucas slid down in his seat a bit and put his head on Nick's shoulder. Nick turned and kissed Lucas's head. "I'm right here with you. I'm not going anywhere."

"Thank you."

"Should you call your parents?"

Lucas sat up and sniffed. "Suppose I should. But not until we know more. My mom will absolutely panic. I don't want her waiting around for news of the results of his surgery."

"And your dad?"

"He's probably away on some business trip." Lucas put his head back on Nick's shoulder. "I'll phone him after I call my mom. He'll want to know what's happening. Eric is his favorite."

"Why do you say that?"

"Eric was always *all boy*. Dad would take him fishing and hunting. I hated those things."

"So, you didn't end up spending much time with him?"

"He taught me how to work on cars. I liked that. But he spent most of his off time with Eric. When I was fifteen, Dad bought me an old junker car. Said we'd work on it together. Never really happened. A buddy and I ended up restoring it together."

Lucas squirmed against Nick.

"What?" Nick asked.

Lucas lay his hand on Nick's thigh. "Looking back, I think I had feelings for my buddy."

"What was his name?"

"Daniel. He was four years older than me." Lucas laughed. "I would find myself staring at his ass when he was leaning over the engine. Stuff like that. And I loved when he spoke to me."

"Your first gay crush."

"I guess so."

"Lucas Peterson?" A woman in scrubs peered around the room. Lucas leaped to his feet.

"Here."

"Can you come with me please?"

Lucas motioned to Nick. "Can my boyfriend come too?"

"We don't like a lot of extra people back there."

"Please. I need him. I'm freaking out."

"Okay." She nodded her head. "I'll tell them you're both family."

Nick didn't hold Lucas' hand as they followed her. If they were going to pretend to be brothers, holding hands was out. Lucas wasn't sure he could survive without touching Nick, though.

They were led to a waiting room further into the hospital. There were people in hospital beds lining the hallway. Most of them seemed to be seniors.

"Your brother is in surgery already," the woman said. "We needed to rush him in."

"Can you tell us anything about his injuries?" Nick asked.

"He has a couple of fractures and a head injury. He fell from fairly high up. We're worried about internal injuries. His red blood cell levels aren't good. He might be bleeding internally."

"Okay." Lucas sat in a chair and stared straight ahead of him.

"Thank you," Nick said to her. When there was no one in the hallway, he reached for Lucas' hand. He brought it over to his lap and held it with both hands.

Lucas felt numb. He couldn't lose his brother. They'd spent most of their young lives together—just them. Eric was his big brother. He needed him in his life.

He glanced over at Nick.

He regretted not telling Eric about Nick. He knew his brother would support him regardless of who he loved. There might have been a few moments of disbelief—maybe even an argument. But his brother would have come around and been happy for him in the end.

He prayed he'd have the opportunity to introduce Nick to him.

Far too many hours went by. It was well past midnight. Nick was keeping them supplied with coffee and snacks. Lucas was exhausted but he couldn't close his eyes. He finally gave in to Nick's urging, stretched out on the chairs, and put his head on Nick's lap.

It was rare that anyone walked down the hallway so they'd given up the brother routine. The waiting room was empty aside from them.

Lucas relaxed as Nick combed his fingers through his hair and used his thumb to brush soothing strokes on his cheek. It was a true extension of love. Nick didn't speak.

He was just there for him.

And it was exactly what Lucas needed.

"Lucas." The woman in the scrubs appeared in front of them. Lucas scrambled to a sitting position. "Your brother is out of surgery. There was some internal bleeding but we think we found it all. As for his bones, he has a compound fracture of his right femur. And the radius and ulna on his left arm are both broken. The head injury, we're concerned about. But time will tell. We'll know more once he wakes up." She placed her hand on Lucas' shoulder. "We have to keep him sedated for now but you can spend a few minutes with him if you'd like."

Lucas leaped to his feet. "Where is he?"

He needed to see him. To see him breathing. To reassure

himself that his brother wasn't gone from his life. Lucas bent down and gave Nick a quick kiss. "Be back in a few minutes."

"Take as long as they'll let you stay," Nick replied.

Lucas followed the woman down the hallway. And then corner after corner until he wasn't sure how to get back to Nick. She led him to a room. It was a little shocking to see his brother like that. Hooked up to so much equipment. He pulled up a chair to his bedside.

"Hey, Eric," Lucas said in case there was any chance Eric could hear him. "You've gone and done it this time. I told you to be more careful."

He reached through the bars and clung to Eric's hand. "I have something to tell you. Someone to tell you about." He rested his forehead on the handrail. "I don't know if you can hear me ... and I should have told you sooner. I should have told you that for the first time in my life, I'm in love."

Eric's chest rose and fell with the help of a machine.

"His name is Nick." Lucas grinned at nothing across the room as tears streamed down his cheeks. "I almost screwed everything up with him. I thought my music was more important. I know it's not now. He's the most important thing in my life. I'd give everything up for him."

Lucas laughed softly. "Don't tell him that. It'll go to his head." He brushed his thumb across Eric's knuckles. "I love him so much. You're going to love him too. He makes me happy. Me. Happy. I know. Hard to believe. Wait until you meet him, though."

Lucas let his gaze wander over his brother's face. It was bruised and it looked as though his cheek was broken. It was swollen and purple, and there was a long incision along it.

"Nick is talented. Music and sound. Intelligent. He's funny and his smile can light up a thousand rooms. He's my perfect match. Kind of a yin and yang situation. I can't imagine life without him." He leaned closer to Eric. "I might even marry him someday."

"Yeah?"

Lucas whipped around. Nick was standing in the doorway with a huge grin on his face. He laughed softly and wandered into the room. He put his hand on Lucas' shoulder.

"The nurse said I could come on down for a few minutes," Nick said.

Nick was talking but Lucas couldn't hear him. His body was buzzing. He'd said it aloud and Nick had heard him say it.

"You weren't supposed to hear that," Lucas said.

"What part? That you can't imagine life without me? Or that you want to marry me someday."

"Either." A rush of heat flushed Lucas' face. "Both."

"You'll have to decide. But I like the idea of both."

Lucas released a long sigh as he tried to regain his breath. "It's too soon. We're not there yet."

Nick kissed the top of Lucas' head. "I said I liked the *idea* of both. I didn't say anything about doing it right away. We can take all the time we need to get there."

Lucas' heart thudded in his ears. "But that's where we're headed?"

"I think so."

"Then my brother has to wake up." Lucas turned back toward Eric. "He has to meet you. It wouldn't be the same if he wasn't my best man at our wedding."

Nick laughed. "You picking out groomsmen already?"

"No." Lucas shook his head. "You're right. I'm jumping ahead."

Nick massaged Lucas' shoulders. "I think it's adorable."

"Can we not bring it up again until we're ready?"

"Agreed." Nick brushed his fingers through Lucas' hair. "I spoke to a doctor out in the hall. They won't be taking him off the sedatives until tomorrow afternoon. Maybe we could go home and get some sleep? You're exhausted and they won't let you stay in his room all night."

Lucas wanted to stay. To sleep in the chairs in the waiting room. But Nick was right. He could barely stand. The stress of the accident, the not knowing, the staying up long past when he would normally be in bed—it was draining him. He wanted to be fresh when Eric woke up. To be by his side and alert to talk to the doctors. He could sleep and come back in the morning.

And Nick had said *home*.

Let's go home as if they lived together.

It gave him a little shiver of warmth.

He nodded his head. "Okay." And dragged himself to his feet. He didn't consciously walk down the hall. Or find his truck in the parking garage. He let Nick lead him.

Time passed in a blur and then they were staring at the front of his house through the windshield. He jumped when Nick opened the passenger door beside him.

"Come on, babe," Nick said. "Let's get you to bed."

Nick held his hand into the house and down to the bedroom. He let Nick undress him and guide him to the bed. He crawled under the covers and curled up against Nick's side.

The sound of Nick breathing. The scent of him. The feel of his embrace.

Whispered words of love as they clung to each other.

This was home.

Chapter Ten | Nick

With Eric out of the ICU, Lucas was able to stay by Eric's side overnight. The couch in the room could be disassembled and turned into a single bed. Eric had been in and out of consciousness and wasn't fully aware of his surroundings, but they'd taken him off the ventilator.

Nick wandered into the room with a coffee, a bran muffin, and a clean set of clothes for Lucas. There was a shower in the bathroom in Eric's room and Lucas had been given permission to use it. Nick's timing was perfect. Lucas was standing in the bathroom in a towel, showered.

"Here's some clean clothes." Nick set them on the counter. "How's Eric?"

"He woke up for a bit this morning and the doctor did some cognitive tests on him. It looks like the head injury didn't do any damage to his brain."

"That's fantastic." Nick rubbed his hand up and down Lucas' bare back. He looked in the mirror. Lucas was exhausted. The firm bed hadn't provided him with much sleep.

"My parents are coming in today." Lucas turned and held Nick's face in one hand. "I can't wait for them to meet you. Are you going to stick around?"

"Of course." Nick moved in and sealed their lips with a kiss. It was tender and loving. He wanted Lucas to know how much he loved him. To know how this tragedy had bonded them even further. Now, he was going to meet his parents. "Have you told them about me?"

Lucas dropped the towel and pulled on his underwear and pants. "I told them I'm in love." His socks and shoes were next and then his shirt.

Nick put his hand on Lucas' chest. "But not that you're in love with a guy."

"I told them I'm gay. Figured they'd work the rest out for themselves."

"Lucas?" A weak voice.

Lucas pulled away and rushed into the main room. "Eric. I'm right here." He leaned over the handrail and held Eric's hand. "You going to wake up properly for me?"

"Yeah, I'm not as groggy." Eric tried to sit up so Lucas raised the head of his bed. Eric's eye caught Nick standing near the bathroom doorway. "Who's that?"

Nick wondered what Lucas would say.

"That's Nick. My boyfriend. The man I'm in love with."

That pretty much covered everything. Nick approached the beside.

"Wait," Eric said as his eyebrows rose. "You're bisexual?"

Lucas shook his head. "No, I'm gay."

"But all those women."

"They didn't mean anything to me compared to what I feel for Nick. It wasn't until I met Nick that things started to click together in my brain. I'm not attracted to women."

"What about Angie? You were together for a long time. You were engaged."

"We were faking it. Not sure why. A marriage wouldn't have lasted long."

"I thought you wanted kids?"

Lucas looked at Nick. "Nick and I can have kids if we decide to."

That statement from Lucas made Nick's heart swell. They'd

discussed kids and how they both wanted them. The stringing together of those words, though. *Nick and I can have kids*. It was exhilarating. They really did have a possible future together. That's where they were headed.

Nick smiled at Lucas, letting him know the sentiment warmed him through.

"I don't know," Eric said. "I don't understand it. What do you see in a dude?"

"We fit," Lucas said. "Our wants and needs. Our passions. The way we think. Everything is compatible. Our lives have become intertwined in an unprecedented, meaningful way."

Eric frowned. "But sex …."

"Is amazing," Lucas answered. "It's what I've been craving all my adult life."

Eric shook his head. "That just grosses me out."

Lucas laughed. "Then stop picturing me having sex with my boyfriend."

"It is being deleted as we speak." Eric sighed. "All right." He looked at Nick. "If my brother loves you, you must be a very special guy. I wasn't sure if he'd ever find true love."

Nick put his hands on the guardrail. "It's nice to meet you."

Eric closed his eyes. "Wish it was under better circumstances."

"Me too," Nick said. It looked as though Eric was going to fall asleep again. He turned. There was a commotion at the door. A women in her 60s burst into the room in tears. A man about the same age followed her in, holding her back from making an absolute rush to Eric's bedside.

"My Eric." Lucas moved out of the way so the woman could lean over the bed and pet Eric's head. Eric opened his eyes and smiled at her. These people were obviously his mom and dad. Lucas looked a lot like his dad. That same intense face. Furrowed brow.

"Dad," Lucas said. "This is Nick." He put his arm around Nick's shoulders. "My boyfriend."

His dad's expression didn't change. Maybe his eyes opened a little wider.

"Always knew there was something off about you," his dad said.

"Yeah, I was gay. I didn't realize it until recently."

His dad's jaw muscle under one ear twitched and jumped. "You're sure about this."

"Dad, I'm in love with him. It's real."

His dad sighed. "All right. It's your life." Then he joined his wife at Eric's bedside. That had gone as well as Lucas had expected. He'd told Nick his dad would be stoic about it but not fight him on it. In addition to fixing cars, Lucas had been obsessed with drawing. He'd shown Nick some of the ones he'd kept. Fantasy landscapes with castles and muscular knights with bulges.

How Lucas hadn't known he was gay was anyone's guess.

His dad had obviously suspected.

His mom must have been listening to their conversation because she shot Nick a glance. Not hostile but not entirely warm either as if she still had to make up her mind about him.

Nick would take it as a win. With both of Lucas' parents and his brother.

"Let's give them some space," Nick said. "Let them visit Eric on their own."

He led Lucas out into the hall and they propped themselves against the wall to wait. Lucas would likely spend another night there. By Lucas' account, Eric cried out for him in the night.

"So, your brother doesn't have a girlfriend or anything?"

Nick asked.

"He was married for eleven years. Nice woman except she cheated on him."

"That's rough." Nick nudged Lucas with his shoulder. "You staying here again tonight?"

"No." Lucas shook his head. "I thought I'd go home. Get some proper rest. Eric and I talked about it. He says he'll be fine on his own."

"I'm glad to hear that. You need some sleep."

Lucas' gaze met Nick's. "Will you come home with me?"

"I'd love to go home with you." Nick gave Lucas a long, sultry kiss. Lucas responded, placing one hand on the small of Nick's back and dragging him closer.

They pulled apart when a nurse walked down the hallway.

"I think I need your touch before I go to sleep," Lucas said.

Nick grinned. "That can be arranged."

"Just let me say goodbye to Eric and my parents." Nick was reluctant to release Lucas. Their hands stayed joined until Lucas was too far away. He could hear Lucas telling Eric he would be back in the morning to see him. Then a curt goodbye to his parents.

It only took them twenty minutes to get to Lucas' house. It took less than a minute for them to get all of their clothes off. They dove into bed together and curled up under the covers.

"Where do you want me to touch you?" Nick teased.

"Let's start with everywhere."

"Mm. That suits me perfectly." Nick ducked beneath the blankets. He went straight for Lucas' cock. He'd been craving it. Dreaming about it. Touching himself at the thought of it.

He sucked its length into his mouth, using his tongue to play with his cockhead. It was thick and firm in his mouth. He held Lucas' waist with both hands as he bobbed on his cock. It felt good on his tongue. He swallowed the cap and buried his nose in Lucas' dense pubes.

He smelled so good.

Nick coughed and withdrew. He sucked him root to tip and pumped him a few times with his hand. "Where to next?" he asked Lucas.

"Let me roll over and I'll show you," Lucas answered.

"Oh … yum." Nick moved out of the way so Lucas could flip over onto his front. He grinned as Lucas got up on his knees, chest to the bed.

Sweet.

Full access.

Nick clapped his hands onto Lucas' ass, spread his cheeks, and dove in. It wasn't long until Lucas's hole opened for him while Lucas groaned and stroked his cock.

Nick lay on the bed beside Lucas. He pumped his hard cock a few times.

"Did you get tested like I suggested when we were together before?" Nick asked.

"Yeah, I got my results a couple of days after we broke up. Negative."

"Me too."

Nick didn't want to ask this next question. It would break his heart if Lucas said yes.

"Were you with anyone when we were broken up?" Nick asked.

"No. You?"

"No."

"So, those two guys were the first people you decided to have sex with?"

Nick laughed. "Seemed like a good idea at the time." He stroked his cock a few more times. "Bring the lube and come here." He patted his thighs. It was one of his favorite positions.

Lucas was quick to straddle him. "We're doing this without a condom?"

"You like that idea?"

"Absolutely prefer it." Lucas winked at him. "I'll be dripping with you."

Nick groaned and pumped his cock harder. That was a picture and a half. His cum drooling down the inside of Lucas' thighs. He let Lucas take over stroking with the lube.

It already felt better without being encased.

Lucas tossed the lube to one side and raised his ass and moved forward. He reached behind him and grasped Nick's cock. He rubbed the head around his hole.

He leaned forward and kissed Nick, then descended on his cock. Inch by inch until he was sitting on Nick's lap. The warmth and the tightness were incredible. Every nerve ending in his cock was firing off. He'd never been in a relationship long enough before to go bareback.

Lucas shifted, rising, and Nick clutched Lucas' thighs.

Jeezus.

He was going to have trouble not cumming right away. Lucas started a steady rhythm up and down, intermittingly seating himself and grinding circles around Nick's cock. Nick gripped Lucas's hips and concentrated on restraint. He didn't want this to end anytime soon.

His cock had never experienced such absolute bliss.

Lucas reached forward and fed Nick this thumb. Nick moaned as he sucked on it and traveled to a place of pure ecstasy. Lucas had taken him there.

Lucas had always taken him there.

Lucas hooked his thumb on Nick's bottom teeth, removed his thumb from Nick's mouth, and placed both of his hands on

Nick's chest. He used his thighs to drill his ass on Nick's cock.

He threw his head back, groaned, and swore.

So loud.

So male.

Lucas continued to bump up and down. Lucas' voice got louder as he grabbed his cock and jerked it hard. Nick felt Lucas' ass clench around his bare cock. Every little sensation traveled through him to his gut. A tight strangle, then Lucas convulsed, grunted, and came on Nick's belly.

"Fuck." Lucas leaned forward and kissed Nick. A sexy, hungry kiss. He reluctantly pulled away and went back to riding Nick's cock. Lucas' eyes looked like he'd been freshly fucked.

His pupils were blown wide. He was sweating with the effort. Nick ran his hands up to Lucas' chest and caressed it. He twisted Lucas' nipples and Lucas' ass clenched in response.

"Cum for me," Lucas whispered. "Fill me up."

Those were the words he needed to hear.

Nick closed his eyes. His back arched and he went back to Lucas' hip with his hands. He needed to cling on tight to keep himself connected to reality. He dug his fingers into Lucas' flesh and came hard. Again—and again. He didn't remember ever cumming that much.

Lucas was going to be dripping with him.

He wanted more.

"Babe, hands and knees," Nick said.

Lucas was quick to respond. Nick positioned himself behind him. His cum was running in a rivulet from Lucas' hole, down his taint, and in a lazy line down between his balls. Forming a teardrop of liquid ready to drip off. Nick chased it back up to Lucas' hole with his thumb.

He stuck his finger in Lucas' hole. Lucas groaned as he

fingered him. Everywhere Nick could feel, Lucas' insides were slick. Nick rose to his knees and fed his cock back into Lucas' hole.

He had enough of an erection left to slide in and out. His cock was sensitive but he wanted to make sure his cum was pushed back high into Lucas' body.

Lucas' hole was gaping and rimmed in white each time Nick pulled out.

He reached through Lucas' legs. Lucas was getting hard again.

"Stay where you are," Nick said, then lay on his back and wormed his way between Lucas' thighs. He licked his balls, then sucked Lucas' cock into his mouth.

Lucas made the most incredible sound.

Nick used one hand to keep Lucas' cock in place. With the other, he found Lucas' hole again and pressed two fingers into it. As he sucked his cock, he fucked Lucas with his fingers.

It wasn't long until Lucas came down his throat.

After a moment to collect themselves, they tumbled back to the head of the bed, laughing.

"Babe," Lucas exclaimed. "That was amazing."

Nick rolled and kissed Lucas, then cupped Lucas' face, and stared into his eyes. "We fit so well with each other. I don't think anyone else could ever take your place."

"I should hope not." Lucas smirked.

"No, I'm being serious." Nick touched Lucas' lips until Lucas relaxed them. "No one … ever. On the drive home, I was thinking about your brother. How you almost lost him."

Lucas brushed his fingers through Nick's hair.

"I don't ever want to lose you," Lucas said.

"I'm not going anywhere." Nick sighed. "And that's what I was thinking about. I'm never going anywhere without you."

He wasn't sure how to phrase this. He just knew he had to.

"What's the matter?" Lucas looked concerned. That hadn't been his intention. He needed to gather every ounce of courage he had access to.

"Nothing. That's the thing. Everything is perfect between us."

"I'm not following."

Nick drew a line down through Lucas' chest hair. "What you said in the hospital room."

"What thing?" Lucas scowled and then his eyebrows raised. "Marriage?"

"Yeah." Nick brushed his lips across Lucas'. He needed to be near him. This was monumental. He needed his best friend near him. "I think I'm ready."

"Think?" Lucas squeezed Nick's arm.

Nick met Lucas' gaze. "I know. I know I'm ready."

Lucas was silent. His scowl told Nick, that Lucas was thinking. Lucas pulled away from him and Nick just about had a heart attack until Lucas kneeled on the mattress facing him.

"I don't have a ring," Lucas said.

Streams of Nick's tears were already flowing. With no glasses and the tears obscuring his vision, Nick could barely see a thing. He reached for and touched Lucas' hands. "I don't care."

"You're my everything, Nick. You helped me find myself. I can never thank you enough for that. I can't imagine being anywhere else but in your arms. Nick … I want to be your husband."

Nick struggled to his knees in front of Lucas. He cleared enough tears to be able to make out Lucas' face. He fully grasped both of Lucas' hands in his. "And I want to be yours."

Lucas grinned. "Fuck, I love you."

"You're the man who keeps my heart beating."

Nick pulled Lucas back to the sheets and curled up facing him. He was sure the rhythms of their hearts were beating as one. He'd found his forever in Lucas.

Chapter Ten | Lucas

~ Six Months Later ~

The audience was loving it. The dance floor was filled with people having a great time. Lucas looked over at Nick. He was smiling and rocking back and forth to the music as he played his guitar. Lucas launched into singing the chorus, strumming his guitar. Nick added harmony to the song with his voice. They'd been told their voices sounded amazing together.

It hadn't surprised them. Everything else fit with them. Even combining households. A week after they decided to marry, Nick had moved in with him. They'd been married four months later.

After Nick moved in, he insisted Lucas give up his construction job. It was too dangerous. They'd almost lost his brother to the profession. With the amount of money Nick made from his sound jobs and both their musical ventures, they were good for money.

Lucas didn't need to be risking his life.

The first change had been to create a band that only played originals. Lucas' and Nick's. And songs they'd worked on together. Their styles complemented each other.

They'd named the band Rhythmic Bliss because that's how they felt about their relationship. They were in sync with everything they did. And their love bordered on transcendent.

They'd brought on a drummer and bass guitar player for that venture. On the side to make extra money, they had a duo group that played all over the city. Lucas on vocals. Nick on guitar.

They spent their days collaborating on music. Nick had set up his sound studio in the second bedroom. He helped independent musical artists get their songs on streaming services.

They spent their nights in each other's arms. Holding, kissing—making love.

Nick finished the last guitar solo of the night.

"That's us for tonight, folks," Lucas said to the crowd. "Get home safe." He backed up and started untangling himself from the in-ear monitors and guitar cable. They managed to break down and store everything in their car in twenty minutes. Enough time to run down to the pub at the bottom of the square and watch a friend's band that was playing until one.

They dashed in the door of the pub winded but laughing.

The lead singer of the band performing spotted them in the crowd on the dance floor. He finished the song he was singing. He pointed at Lucas and Nick.

"We have some awesome musicians in the audience tonight. Put your hands together and maybe we can get them up here to sing something."

The clapping, hoots, and hollers were deafening. Lucas and Nick, both grinning, held hands as they found their way onto the stage. Nick approached the lead singer and whispered what song they wanted to do. The lead singer told the rest of the band and Nick told Lucas.

Lucas took the lead spot and Nick sang harmony.

When they finished the song, the crowd cheered—and went insane with exuberance when Lucas grabbed Nick's face and kissed him.

They left the stage laughing.

This was the life they loved.
Music, love—and absolute bliss.

Dear Reader

I hope you enjoyed reading *Rhythmic Bliss*.

Please take a moment to review this book on the website of the store where you purchased your copy of *Rhythmic Bliss*.

If you would like to touch base and say hello to the author, you can email them at: leigh@leighjarrett.com

About the Author

Leigh Jarrett (she/he) is an unabashedly queer, quirky, and passionate author of Contemporary MM+ Romantic Fiction. Their published contemporary works include warm and always sexy HEA romances as well as dark romances filled with grit, trauma, and angst.

In their hometown of Victoria, BC, Canada, Leigh can be found nestled up with their fabulously supportive wife and trusty laptop or enjoying the wondrous Vancouver Island outdoors.

Please consider subscribing to Leigh's newsletter to stay up to date with their new releases and promos. If you're interested in MM+ Fantasy and Paranormal Romance, check out one of Leigh's other pen names, JT Fader, on their JT Fader Fantasticals website and newsletter jtfader.com.

To connect with Leigh Jarrett:

Email: leigh@leighjarrett.com

Website and newsletter: leighjarrett.com

You can also find Leigh on Bluesky

Other Books by Leigh Jarrett

"It all came down to a matter of trust."
A Friends to Lovers M/M Gay Romance
Snowblind

"Find love in the least expected place."
An Enemies to Lovers M/M Gay Romance

Merlot Rebellion

"Risking it all to follow your heart."
A Found Family M/M Bisexual Romance

Capital Adoration

"Brave enough to pursue love."
An Age Gap M/M Gay Romance

Pacific Pursuit

"Learning a new path to love."
A Roommates to Lovers Bisexual Awakening M/M Romance

Academic Adoration

"Recovering true love."
A Second Chance Hurt/Comfort M/M Romance

Drag Undivided